Hey kid! Does she love me?

Harry Mazer

PAN HORIZONS

First published in the United States of America 1984 by
Thomas Y. Crowell Junior Books
This edition first published in Great Britain 1986 by
Pan Books Ltd,
Cavaye Place, London SW10 9PG
© Harry Mazer 1984
9 8 7 6 5 4 3 2 1
ISBN 0 330 29616 7
Phototypeset by Input Typesetting Ltd, London
Printed in Great Britain by
Hunt Barnard Printing, Aylesbury, Bucks

J
23,317M

For the new baby in the house,
MAX RAPHAEL,
and for
JENNY BETH

1

Jeff made a tunnel of his hands, turned himself into a camera's eye, and 'shot' his friend, Danny Belco, as he knelt to weld the pan of a '62 VW Bug. Danny turned the brim of his cap around a couple of times. 'What are you doing?'

'Watching you.'

'You're always watching.'

'You're always doing.'

Danny put on his welding hood. 'Guess who's back in town?'

'Who?' Jeff said.

'Don't you know?'

'What is this, a quiz?'

'Come on, guess.'

It was hot, summer hot. Jeff felt loose limbed, limp, and heavy. Outside the intense light bounced off the side of Danny's house and across the chewed-up lawn and over the woodpile and the dented green van with the four flat tyres where Danny stored spare parts.

Jeff watched the play of muscles across Danny's bare back, the way they jumped and swelled as he worked. Jeff was taller than Danny, with longer arms and legs, but he was also softer. There was a little bulge in the middle when he belted his pants. The muscles were there, but they didn't advertise themselves.

But then, everything about Danny was more defined. From the cars he worked on – only vintage VWs, circa 1960 to 1970 – to the kind of girls he liked. 'She has to be five feet five, exactly two inches shorter than me, have good legs, a small can, and a pair of grapefruit-sized tits that I can hold comfortably.' He'd found her, too. Tracy Stauffer. (Jeff didn't know about the grapefruit part.)

And Jeff? His future was like a cloud that he couldn't grab hold of. It kept changing shape and direction. He'd graduated. Big deal. *Now I am a high school graduate.* He couldn't even say it without mocking himself. *You are a high school graduate. The world beckons. Time to go, time to fly, time to do.* Do what?

Who was he? What was his identity? Director Orloff? Or Jeff Orloff? Jeff Orloff was a slob, wore sweaters with the elbows out, no shirts, never a tie. The knees of his jeans sagged. Ah, but Director Orloff! He wore white turtleneck sweaters, tweed jackets with leather elbows, he had a notebook in one pocket, a copy of *Variety* in the other and his horn-rimmed glasses dangling from his teeth.

Let me introduce myself, Jeff Orloff, World-famous Movie Director. And why not? He was as unqualified as the next guy. Think big. Everyone else did. Weren't the guys who tripped over their own feet all going to be quarterbacks for the Dallas Cowboys, and guys who couldn't do math without counting on their fingers going to be astronauts?

He loved movies. He was a movie freak. He was always making movies in his head and scribbling down ideas for other movies. He'd even shot a couple of videos at school in a course he'd taken. A ghost movie everyone liked. His family, anyway. Last summer he'd taken a job as usher at the Penn Can Mall, just so he could see movies. For one week he tore tickets in half and ogled the girls and swept up the popcorn containers and made the little kids sit down. Good job until the air conditioning activated an allergic coughing attack and ruined a promising career.

Danny's welding arc threw up long, crooked shadows. Through his cupped hands Jeff panned across the high roof. *Long shot:* The inside of the barn, open space, dusty beams. *Angle shot from above:* Circle of light centred on the figure below.

Danny popped up. 'Did you guess yet?' A smile trembled

under his newly planted moustache. Danny, when he was younger, had had a big head and straw-coloured hair. Now that he was older, he had the same hair, the same big, cheerful, teasing face. 'This girl I'm talking about, she's a friend of yours.'

'Which one? Tracy?' asked Jeff with a smile.

'No, not Tracy.' Danny tossed a clamp at Jeff's foot. 'I'm talking about Mary Silver.'

Jeff picked up the clamp and wound it into his hand. Mary Silver. What did Danny know? There was nothing to know. Mary Silver had been a girl in school who went off to college. That's all.

'Mary Silver, Mary Silver,' Danny said. 'Don't look so dumb. You remember her. You have her pictures all over your wall.'

The pictures were from a school production of *Cyrano de Bergerac*. Mary had been Roxanne, and in his fantasy Jeff had been Cyrano, big nose and all.

He searched out the dark corners of the barn, his eyes veering back and forth like a camera. That was the way he used to follow Mary Silver in school, when he was a sophomore and she was a senior – stare after her, watching, watching . . . He'd had a thousand imaginary conversations with her – a thousand clever-stupid ways he'd start talking to her. Maybe tackle her in a football uniform. He was never on any team, but in his head he was on every team. Fielding a baseball, one handed, right in her lap. Oh, excuse me!..His ideas were all a little lascivious.

Once, coming out of school, he'd seen her drop her notebook and all the jerks standing around laughed. He was one of the jerks, but in his mind he was down there helping her. Another time, by the lake during the regatta, he saw her standing near the water and imagined her falling in, clinging to an overturned canoe, white water raging below and he there at the last moment, leaping, flying, snatching her away to a safe place where they would be alone and . . . These scenarios never needed words. They went back to the days of the old silent movies. He was Hairbreadth Harry, In-the-Nick-of-Time Jones, Jeff Hopalong Orloff to the rescue.

He imagined calling her.

MARY: I think you have the wrong number.

JEFF: Oh, sorry, but your voice (*beat*) it's so (*beat*) how should I say it? (*beat*) so special.

MARY: Who is this?

JEFF: An admirer.

MARY: I know who this is. Don't I know you from school?

JEFF: (*modestly*) You may have heard of me. This is Jeff Orloff. (*Music rising: 'The Grand Canyon Suite.'*)

MARY: Jeff Orloff, the movie director? The kid from North High who made it big in Hollywood? (*Fanfare in brass.*)

JEFF: Just call me Jeff. (*Famous, but unspoiled.*)

He'd actually called her once. Called his own bluff. He'd written the whole dialogue out in his looseleaf notebook. *Hi, Mary? This is Jeff Orloff, I've seen you around school, would you like to go to a movie Saturday? You would? Great! See you then.*

When she actually answered the phone, he froze. 'Hello?' she said. He forgot his dialogue. He stood there, gripping the phone, dripping sweat, squeezing the handle into a fruity pulp. 'Hello?' He couldn't hang up, couldn't speak. He was like an insect pinned in space, suspended between heaven and hell. He tried not to breathe. Did she guess it was him? Jeff Orloff, the heavy-breathing pervert. Finally, she hung up. Afterward, for a long time he was afraid to look her way even for a second, for fear that she'd catch a whiff of his pervert breath.

After Mary graduated and went away to college, he was aware of her without thinking about her, without hope or anything like that. She became part of a vague wanting, a hidden part of himself he didn't talk about to anyone. Things that were gone, things that were lost, things that would never be. What a great athlete he'd be. How much money he'd make – a million before he was twenty. Kid thoughts, kid desires. The sort of things that made people laugh. Desires that he kept out of sight in some attic of his mind, like toys he no longer played with but still wished he could.

'It's summer,' he said. 'Why shouldn't Mary Silver be here? She lives here, doesn't she?'

'You don't know anything, do you? Her family moved to Florida last year.'

How did Danny know that? Why was he bringing up Mary? 'Maybe she's visiting. She's probably visiting friends.'

'Yeah.' Danny gave Jeff his big homely smile. 'Visiting.' He pulled the welding lines around the pan. 'With her baby.'

Jeff shielded his eyes against the sparking electric arc.

'Baby,' Danny repeated. 'B-A-B-Y. Baby.'

'Is she married?'

'Do you need a licence to do it? She was here yesterday, talking to Mom. She's going to live here.'

Jeff spun the clamp in his hand. That was the first thing he'd heard that he could understand. The Belcos rented rooms.

'I told Mom, Mary could have my room. With me in it.'

Jeff tossed the clamp at Danny.

'Hey! Where are you going?' Danny called. 'Jeff, you idiot, you just got here. What difference does it make to you, anyway?'

2

The first time Jeff saw Mary Silver was in a school play three years ago. He was a sophomore, she was a senior. He couldn't remember the name of the play, but he never forgot Mary. On the stage, something extraordinary happened – it had to do with her face, her eyes, the way she moved, the natural way she acted. She wasn't acting. She *was* the character. Nobody else on that stage came near her. She was in a class by herself.

Watching her, he was awed and inspired. It was just a high school play and she was just a student who went to good old North High, an ordinary school like ten thousand others. This wasn't New York or Hollywood High. This was nowhere. But there was Mary, like a star in that dumb little play. He'd see her in the halls, watch her with her friends, and think a queen was passing by with her retinue.

It wasn't that she was beautiful – she was short and slight and her mouth was wide, her nose was just a nose, and her hair hung the way most hair does. But her eyes – ah, her eyes! They were large, like two fat eggs . . . *Cut!* Can't you say it better than that, Orloff? Two dark pools . . . *Cut!* In writing movie dialogue, less is more, Orloff.

> JEFF: Your eyes . . .
> MARY: My eyes?
> JEFF: Your eyes . . . Ahhh . . .

When he learned her name, Silver, and that she lived over on Rugby Road, he thought she was English. She had that smooth creamy colour, those expressive eyes. Maybe Irish. He never guessed Jewish.

Mary's father was a doctor. The Silvers lived in a brick and timber Tudor-style house across from the cemetery. After he saw her in the play, he remembered that her father,

Dr. Silver, had come to the school once in junior high and talked to them about the Holocaust. What Jeff remembered was the part where her father said that, during the Second World War in Poland, he and his sister hid behind a false partition in back of a pantry in a Christian home.

Because of Mary, Jeff joined the Drama Club. They should have tossed him out. He was the worst actor in the club, and he was always arguing with Mr. Farah. Plays were so talky, unlike movies. He wanted more action, more tension, more visual stuff. Anything Mr. Farah did, Jeff had another idea. 'I need to make a statement,' he said one day. That's the kind of pompous ass he was, but Mr. Farah never laughed. 'This is the way I see the part,' Jeff would say. 'Let the character show himself more in action and less in talk.'

'Interesting point of view, Orloff,' Mr. Farah would say, 'but it's not the way I see it.' When Jeff was carrying on, the other kids stood around giving him the gong sign. He didn't dare look at Mary. Never spoke to her. He, whose mouth runneth over, couldn't say a word to her. When they passed in the hall, she smiled. But then, she was the star. She probably smiled at everyone.

Mary. Mary Silver. Mary Silver back in town? Mary Silver, with a baby? He couldn't make the connection, but connections were all he thought about. To make a baby, there had to be a connection – two people, a man and a woman. Sex, that was the connection he was stuck on. Sex, Mary, and this guy who gave her the baby.

He told himself to raise his horizons, get his mind out of the gutter. What business was it of his if Mary Silver had a baby? She didn't owe him any explanations. Whatever she did, she did. Butt out, Orloff, back off. But his mind had a mind of its own.

The next day, he was almost at Danny's house when he remembered what Danny had said. Mary was moving into the Belco house. Was she there now? He walked down

Spring Street, imagining her at the window, behind the curtains, watching him. He kept going, went by the house like he was on a stage, walking tall and straight, ass tight, swinging along, getting that rhythm, that jive into his shoulders.

He crossed Carbon with its crowded little houses and went past the dark, half-abandoned factories along Wolf, then down Park Street under the highway and the new construction, past the dust-covered car lots and the mud and flowers where the sidewalk ended. He walked along the shoulder of the parkway with the lake on his left till he got to the hill above the French Fort, where he sat and peered through the circle of his fingers. Framed, focused, concentrated. Blotting out the rusting railroad bridge, the polluted lake, and the hokey-looking little fort that not even the tourists came to.

There was another world here once before the chimneys and gas tanks. Trees once surrounded the lake, and huge fish swam in its waters – salmon and sturgeon and trout. He saw it all, his eye at the centre, a darting brown eye, moving here and here and here – a director's eye.

Ancient smoke rose from the stone chimneys. He smelled the wood fires and heard the hubbub – pigs and dogs, the tumult inside. Canoes approached. Indian canoes bringing furs for barter and a white woman and her baby. He saw them from the hill above the fort, where he rested, his arm on his long flintlock. The scout Orloff, with an eagle feather in his handband.

Cut! This was the white woman's story – Mary's story. How she was returned to her people after years of captivity. She wasn't going to be accepted . . . not with her Indian papoose. Her life was going to be miserable. But rescue was near. There was that man on the hill, the loner, the trapper, the scout Orloff . . .

Cut! There he was thinking of himself again. This was Mary's story. She had the problem, not him. But he

14

couldn't think about her without thinking about himself. He was at the centre of every story he created. Face it, Orloff, you're self-absorbed.

Were his ideas worth anything? He could never make his mind up about himself. Was he Jeff Orloff, World Splitter, the Abe Lincoln of the Universe? Or Jeff Orloff, a Spit in the Ocean? Ordinary, like all the other ordinaries. That's why he loved the movies. What happened in the movies was never ordinary. Movie makers knew that ordinary life was too boring, too uninteresting. Jeff Orloff, movie maker. He liked the sound of it.

But the next moment his doubts returned. What had he done? Hung around the Drama Club. Read a bunch of movie scripts. Played around with a video camera. Who was he kidding?

But a wise man once said everybody was nobody once.

Now you're talking.

Like a damn fool. Your head is too big, if you ask me.

Tell me, Orloff, what are these important, imposing ideas in your head? What are these great things you want to do?

Be famous. Get rich. Have a stable of Jeff Orloff groupies.

His grandfather was born in Russia, but he was born here. Fame was what America was all about. Fame was what America looked up to. He who climbed to the top of the ant heap ruled the world.

He was going to get there, up there in the light, with all the other world masters, where nobody's shadow would fall across his. He'd stand among the noted directors of the world. Yes, and that was when Mary Silver would see him.

3

Thursdays and Fridays, Jeff washed dishes downtown near City Hall at Sadie's Diner. Now that he was out of school, he worked straight through from six in the evening to six in the morning. Between Sadie's, painting the house for his father, and helping Danny on the garbage truck, he was beginning to accumulate money, his getaway money, his California-Here-I-Come money. He kept the loot in a square red metal box that used to hold imported butter cookies from Denmark. When he'd started, the money had fallen to the bottom. Now he had to push the bills down to close the lid.

He'd never saved before in his life. Money was magic. When you needed it, it appeared. Money was something your parents gave you. But no more. His father said it. 'Go to school or go to work. Don't expect any handouts.' Saving, accumulating, talking about money, figuring all the time – that was something his parents did. And now he was doing it, too.

Danny's mother, Mrs. Belco, had helped get him the job at Sadie's. Star Taxi, where she worked, was across the street from Sadie's. When the taxi business was slow, Mrs. Belco, wearing her yellow Star Taxi slicker, would hang out at the diner, nursing a cup of coffee. Sometimes, when she worked through the night, she drove Jeff home.

Sadie was a large woman with a round, sweaty face. She'd built up Sadie's from a small, shabby diner to one of the most popular restaurants downtown. 'I did it all myself,' she told Jeff. 'I know this business backward and forward and inside out. Nobody fools me.' She fixed her sharp triangular eyes on Jeff. 'The dishwasher before you thought he was fooling me. He was serving himself strip sirloin steaks and Heineken beer for his meal.'

'Orloffs only eat cheese sandwiches and root beer.' If Sadie got the joke, she didn't show it.

The good thing about working all night was that Sadie usually went home after the supper rush. Around midnight, after the movie crowd left and he got the dishwasher loaded, Jeff could relax and go sit out in back where it was cool, or if Danny came down, they'd have pie and ice cream at the counter and watch the customers. That was Jeff's favourite pastime. 'Night people aren't like day people,' he said to Danny.

'Look the same to me.'

'Night people are more interesting.'

'If you're talking about women—'

Ah, the women! Jeff had always had girlfriends, even a few intense relationships, but the diner at night was something else. Women kept coming in out of the dark, in pairs mostly or in groups, looking dazed and blinking their eyes like moths that couldn't get used to the light. They'd been to the movies or bars and they'd order coffee and . . .

Jeff would recommend Sadie's famous homemade strawberry shortcake. 'It's the best in the city.' And then he'd ask what movie they'd seen. 'How did you like it? Isn't Streep great? What'd you think of the directing?'

'He knows movies,' Danny would say. 'Everything, way back to the beginning. You can ask him anything.'

One time a couple of women came in and struck up a conversation. The four of them hit it off. Michelle, the one Jeff liked, had gone to North High. And her girlfriend, who was wearing three pairs of earrings, loved VWs. Jeff said he had to work till six in the morning, but if Ellen drove around to the parking lot in back, the four of them could have a party.

For days afterward, Jeff kept looking for them to come back, but they never did.

Mornings when Sadie came in from the farmer's market, Jeff would unload the truck. It was the last thing he did before he went home. 'You want me to do anything else?' Sadie was at a table out front looking over accounts and talking to Mrs. Belco.

'Who's the good-looking kid, Sadie?' Mrs. Belco gave him a wink. She always teased him when she was with Sadie. 'You ought to come over to my house sometime, Sadie. It's full of cute boys.'

'What I need, Marie, is not a boy.' Sadie glanced up from the bills she was checking. 'You unload the truck yet?' Those narrow eyes doubted everything.

'Everything's in the cooler.'

'Not the fruit. I told you. Bring the fruit out front, where the customers can see it.'

'That's where it is.'

In the cab, Mrs. Belco wanted to know why he hadn't come to the house all week. 'Mrs. Brown said you were supposed to bring her the TV magazine.'

'I've been busy.' The truth was that since finding out that Mary was living at the Belcos', he was staying away. 'I'm painting our house for my father. Tell her I'll bring it over later today.'

'Later today means today, Jeff, not next week. She's an old lady. She doesn't have forever.'

He went over to the Belcos' late that afternoon. 'Hello?' The door was unlocked and he went in and upstairs, half expecting, half afraid, to see Mary. He hammered on Mrs. Brown's door. 'It's me, Jeff. I brought you your magazine.'

Mrs. Century – his private name for her – opened the door a crack. He caught a whiff of sewing machine oil and the dusty smell of cloth. Even in this summer heat she kept her windows closed.

'Your *TV Guide*,' he shouted.

'Jeffrey.' Mrs. Century gripped his arm and pulled him into the room. He was company and he had to sit in the best chair and take some hard candies from a glass jar. The sewing machine was open, and next to it the bed was piled high with cloth. She made aprons for a volunteer group, patched all the Belcos' clothes, and was proud of the way she could still bend and read a tape.

She pushed a chair up next to his, locking him in with her cane. 'How do you like our new boarder? She has a baby with her. Two little babies. That's what they are. Isn't it awful what people do these days? How many candies did you take? That's not enough, a big boy like you. Take more, Jeffrey. I know how you boys love sweets. I haven't forgotten. I had a little boyfriend who used to bring me candy all the time. I loved lemon drops especially, and he'd bring me little root beer barrels and redhots.' She puckered up her mouth. 'Cinnamony and hot. Do you still have them?'

'I think so, Mrs. Brown.'

She shook her head. 'They're gone, I know it. Everything's gone. I'm the only old relic left. My doctor says I can't eat anything sweet any more because of my diabetes.'

'Mrs. Brown,' he said, raising his voice. 'I'm sorry, I have to go.'

'What's on TV? Nothing but crook shows. Crooks and cops. I only like to watch in the afternoon. Such nice stories, such lovely people. At night it's so much violence. I can't sleep afterward. I never used to be that way. The minute my head touched the pillow I was asleep, and I could eat anything I wanted and I used to go everyplace. Now I never leave this room. I feel I'm getting stale, my mind, I can't read any more, and the news on television . . .' She laughed. 'Listen to the old lady complain. Don't get old. You won't like it. It's very unpopular.'

Jeff felt sorry for her because she was old and alone and didn't have anybody to talk to. So he sat and listened to the same things he'd heard before.

'Yes, Mrs. Cen—Mrs. Brown . . .' He'd been nodding

off, it was so warm in her room. A noise in the hall made him shiver. It was just a whisper of a sound. Was it Mary? Was she going to come bursting into the room? That's the way he thought of her, the star making her entrance. My beloved fans . . . He smelled something, a warm, powdery smell. The baby? Then he heard footsteps on the stairs . . .

'I'm going to be ninety-one this October,' Mrs. Century said. She put her hand on his arm. 'I know, I don't look a day over a hundred.' She paused to see if he got the joke.

Later he heard Mary – was it Mary? – going back upstairs. He sat and listened till he heard a door close, and then he left.

4

His father stood in the hall outside Jeff's room, clearing his throat . . . 'Chhrrrup! Chhrrrup!' He had been doing this every day since Jeff graduated high school.

'Jeff, the Russians are coming.'

'Uhhhr.'

'The Russians are coming.'

'Uhrrr.'

'You are awake?'

'Uhrr.'

'Jeff.'

'I'm up!' Jeff thrashed around, knowing this wasn't enough, knowing his father wouldn't be satisfied till he got out of bed, opened the door, and showed himself in person, on his feet, in the flesh. When he was little, his father would sit at the edge of his bed every night and tell him stories while Jeff's mother straightened the room. His parents had three children, but he was the only one at home. They'd had the first two fast and then waited twelve years before they had Jeff. He'd grown up like an only child with four parents.

At fourteen Jeff had declared his independence. Out went the wagon-wheel bed frame, curtains, the brown and tan rug with the cowboy and lasso motif. Down went the mattress to the floor, up went the movie posters – Humphrey Bogart in *The Maltese Falcon* over his mattress, the Marx Brothers in *A Night at the Opera* between the windows, King Kong on the ceiling. Outside his door a triangular sign warned: RADIOACTIVE AREA. ALL UNAUTHORIZED PERSONNEL KEEP OUT.

His mother tried to save the curtains. He stuck to the old army blankets he'd tacked up. Lying close to the floor, the stereo next to his ear, he felt the whole room vibrate, imagined that the house was vibrating, too, shaking the foundation loose, shaking him loose from this old world, jetting him out of the chimney to another life, his true world where he would be reshaped, reformed, reconstituted like Tang or Carnation Instant Dry Milk, a new product, a new order, a new being.

No longer did his father step inside Jeff's room. He said just a sniff of it raised his blood pressure to dangerous levels.

This is their morning scene. The father waits in the hall. The son emerges for inspection in his underwear, after carefully checking for stains and dubious marks. The father polite, careful, but unable to keep the disappointment from his furrowed brow.

Today he said, 'You're up. Good. It's good to be up in the morning. I want to talk about today's business. You're painting today, is that correct?'

'Yes, sir.' His father appreciated a crisp military response.

'Good, I want you to concentrate on the back of the house today. But be careful. Ladders can slip. Stake the bottom before you go up.'

Does his father have to wake him up to tell him this? His father starts Jeff's acid juices flowing, the frothy red, the scratchy crabs of dissatisfaction and impatience. He is angry at his father for treating him like a moron. He is angry at himself for listening. His father lacks confidence in him, doesn't respect him. But instead of telling his father to back off (he wishes he could), he stiffens to attention, hiding his disrespect with excessive politeness.

'Yes, sir,' he says. Yes, my commanding officer. His father has a love affair with the military, having been in the United States Army Air Force, an officer and a bombardier during World War II. The Big One. His father enjoys playing Army. Every morning his father shaves, then waxes the ends of his moustache to a fine point. He has thick wavy hair and a square face. When he's dressed for work he looks like a dashing British colonel – Alec Guinness in an English movie – lacking only a swagger stick. Except that his father's swagger stick is a yellow clipboard. He's an expeditor in a factory, chasing orders and parts and doing payrolls. His father's father – Jeff's grandpa – had worked in that same factory, but on the production floor. Being in the office, his father is part of management, but barely. His father's office is still on the factory floor, and Big Management is upstairs.

His father isn't what he appears to be. He looks convivial, like a mixer, like a man with a lot of friends, but in fact he keeps to himself, puttering around the house or yard till it's dark and then reading till bedtime. He doesn't have *any* friends that Jeff is aware of. It's all family.

How has his father stayed with that one job all these years without getting bored out of his mind? Has he ever wanted to do anything else? Does he feel his life has been wasted? Does it make him sad? Isn't that why he twirls and curls his moustache and cultivates a daring look? Is Jeff going to end up like his father?

'Are you listening?'

'Yes, sir.'

'What does that mean? Are you being sarcastic?'

'No, it means I'm going to cooperate to the best of my ability. To the utmost. I'll start at the top of the peak today. I'm going to work my ass off,' Jeff says, then, wanting to give his father something, he adds generously, 'I'll probably finish the whole side today. If it doesn't rain.'

His father lays a hand on Jeff's shoulder. 'I want you to be careful on that ladder, Jeff. I don't want you to get hurt.'

Jeff's playfulness runs right out of him. His father's concern, the warmth of his hand gets him right in the bones. His father loves him, cares about him, worries about him. Why is he such an ingrate? His father is doing the best he can. What does his father have to look forward to? What opportunities remain? Retirement, and then he'll sit around for the rest of his life. Which could be a long time. The Orloffs were a healthy lot of barnyard animals.

After his father left, he went back to bed, lay on his stomach, then on his side, tangled his legs in the sheet, but couldn't get back to sleep. He thought about the Late Show he'd watched last night, Hitchcock's *The Thirty-Nine Steps*. A classic. He'd seen it seven times already. The scenes when Robert Donat is on the run were his favourites. The way he got away from the police on the train by stepping into Madeleine Carroll's compartment – so smooth. 'Darling . . .' Everything with a smile, embracing and kissing her as the police peer in.

Darling . . . It was him and Mary Silver, his charm overcoming her distrust and suspicion.

He hardly knew her. It had been years since he'd seen her. He'd never even talked to her. Why couldn't he stop thinking about her? He couldn't. It was an obsession. That was interesting. He was obsessed with Mary Silver. He wanted to see her. He had to see her. He was desperate to see her.

He got up finally and put on his white work pants. He loved to be in his pants. He should never stand in front of his father in his underwear. It put him at such a disadvantage. There was something so snug and secure, so at home, when he was zippered up. There was a pleasure in taking off his pants – something erotic and a little exciting, but also a little unnerving. He felt exposed, slightly vulnerable. Oddly, it was in locker rooms that he felt the most vulnerable. Around other males there was always a judgment going on. Am I adequate? Barely adequate? Outstanding? Enviable?

When he put on his pants, when he was in them, zipped up and buttoned, it was like being in his room. At home in his pants. No anxiety, no worried thoughts. He was in the privacy of his own pants and, as everyone knew, a man's pants were, so to speak, his castle.

His mother was in the dining room looking over her lesson plans. She was still in her jogging suit. She was a history teacher at one of the suburban high schools. She was teaching summer school. She always had to have something to do. She was a runner, a spare, energetic woman, not an extra ounce on her.

'Do you want me to make your breakfast?' she said.

'No, I'll take care of myself.'

'I put everything out for you.'

'Watch this. Time me.' Jeff waited till his mother checked her watch, then cracked a couple of eggs in a pan, adjusted the flame, broke open an English muffin, popped it in the toaster, poured juice and a glass of milk.

She tapped her watch. 'Two minutes and forty-five seconds. No, make that forty-four. I think it's an all-time record, Jeff.'

'I've got to do better. You ought to see Chris, the morning chef at Sadie's. I'm studying him. Once I learn the hot griddle, I'll always be able to get a job. Pays pretty good, too.'

A long, pregnant pause. Papers rustled, pages were turned. She didn't like to hear him talk about diner jobs. 'What's on the agenda today?' she said.

'I'm painting.'

His mother started clearing the table. 'Anything else?'

'Isn't that enough?' He sopped up the remains of the egg with the muffin and took his milk down in one swallow. 'If you must know, I am going to the movies when I'm done.'

'In the middle of the day?'

'Why not? I like movies. Besides, they're related to my work.'

'Dishwashing? Or are you going to watch a cooking movie?'

'Yes. A classic. *Gone with the Soup.*'

That got a little smile.

'Why don't you go down to the library this afternoon and check out that little college I told you about? They've got a filmmaking programme. That's why I thought it would be interesting to you.'

'I appreciate that, Ma, but I'm not going to the library. Movies are my school, Mom. I can't be a director if I don't see a lot of movies. For me, movies are like what taking a lab course in chemistry would be for someone else.'

'You think going to college will give you a communicable disease?' She put out her hand. 'Jeff, I know you. You're not going to be satisfied working in a diner for the rest of your life.'

'Who's talking about the rest of my life? I'm ambitious, Mom.' He touched her wrist lightly.

'Your ideas, yours and Dad's, they're fine, but they're yours. They worked for you. They worked for Jules and Natalie. Go to school, find a profession, get a good job. Fine. You've got one lawyer. One psychologist. Two professionals. You're proud. I'm glad. Your third child is ordinary.'

'Stop it, Jeff. You don't believe that, and neither do I. Your mind is every bit as good as your brother's and sister's. Give yourself a chance. Why not go to college for a year, see what it's like?'

'What's the rush? I just graduated high school. I don't want to spend the rest of my life in school.'

'Okay, fine. Then stop lying around the house and get a real job. A full-time job.'

'Okay, I will. Right now, I'm going out to paint, as requested by my father,' he said, underlining each word. 'I am going up on the ladder and I will paint the house. If I don't fall off the ladder today, tomorrow I will paint the driveway side of the house, and if I survive that, the next day the garden side and the day after the front, and then I will be done. And after that I will never ask you or Dad for anything. I will earn all my own money. I will buy my own clothes. I will buy my own food and pay rent. I will not lay around the house.'

'Lie.'

'Liar!' His cheeks burned.

'Lie around, not lay around.'

'Oh . . . what the—' His grammar was being corrected. 'Whatever. I will not ever lay or lie around the house.' He ran water in the sink. 'Nor will I ask anyone to clean up after me. I will clean up my room, I will hang curtains and sleep on a bed. I will work. I will be a model son.' He pressed his lips to his mother's hair, that soft, sweaty earthiness. There was grey in his mother's hair. He loved her tenderly. He also wanted to rap her on the head. 'Forgive me, Mother, I know not what I do.'

She grabbed him by the neck. 'I'd like to strangle you sometimes, my darling son.' She kissed him. 'Go paint.'

Outside, he stripped off his shirt. Paint can in one hand, brush between his teeth, he went up the ladder. He worked the brush down and back and under the clapboard and then smoothly across the face, then down to the next clapboard. Rhythm, rhythm, rhythm . . . not thinking . . . getting into the swing of work, using his body, sweating. Forget trying to figure everything out.

5

Spring Street was quiet. It was still early. The only sounds were the chatter of birds and the hollow regular thump of the newspapers as the news kid came down the street. He tossed Jeff the Belco paper. The house was still asleep. Upstairs the shades were drawn, but there was a light on in an attic room. Mary? Danny had said she was living up there. *Fade in:* Mary looks out her window, sees Jeff. Puzzled, but intrigued. *Cut to Jeff:* A look of recognition. *Quick cuts:* Mary at window. Jeff on sidewalk. Lines flowing between them, a whole net of lines, the two of them caught and tangled in an understanding truer than any words. *Music up*.

Jeff sat on the porch, flipping through the morning paper. Robert, Danny's little brother, came out in his pyjamas. 'Give me the funnies, Jeff.' He was eating a banana. Jeff folded up the paper.

'Where's your brother?'

'Sleeping.'

'Still sleeping?' He went inside. The house was stuffy and dark. From somewhere deep inside he heard a baby cry.

'Jeff, guess this riddle. Why did the robber take a bath?'

'So he could come clean.'

'Wrong. The robber took a bath so he could make a clean getaway.'

'I like my version better.' Jeff went up the carpeted stairs, past Danny's room, then up another flight of stairs to the attic where Vet, another of Mrs. Belco's boarders, also lived. He was just going to see if she was up there.

It was dark, and all the doors were shut. There was a smell of ammonia and after-shave lotion. The baby cried.

It stopped him. He didn't belong here. He backed towards the stairs as a door opened.

'What are you doing up here?' Vet was barelegged, wearing a short red bathrobe, like a boxer, and rubber clogs.

'I heard—' There was an obstruction in Jeff's throat. He was caught where he didn't belong, and he started making excuses. 'I was looking for Danny. I heard a noise . . . I thought Danny—'

'Jeff,' Danny called from below.

Jeff ducked downstairs, sure that Vet had seen right through him.

Danny was tucking in his pants. 'You ready? Where were you? My uncle's out there. Let's go.'

In the truck, Jeff sat by the window, looking out, not saying much. At the first pickup, he and Danny hopped out. Danny worked the back while Jeff heaved the garbage cans up to him. He was glad for the hard work. After a while it got him over the bad feelings.

They took turns, one of them on the ground and the other in the truck, challenging each other to see who could work harder. It was fun for a while, hefting the cans to their shoulders, then tossing them over the rim.

Danny's uncle Val never moved from the driver's seat. 'I used to do the whole job myself,' he told them, looking out, 'until I gave myself a double hernia.' He was a pig farmer over by the Fair Grounds, and he did garbage pickups for markets and restaurants and then fed the garbage to his pigs. 'These pigs eat better than I do.' Jeff had seen them, pink, ugly brutes, up to their bellies in muck.

It was a hot, sweaty job. As the morning went on, the cans got heavier and Jeff's body ran with sweat. He and Danny kept changing places, but towards the end it was just hard work.

The last stop was a fish restaurant on the North Side.

Val went inside to get some fresh walleyes. Danny tossed the last can off the truck, then climbed up in back with some pieces of cardboard for them to stretch out on.

The sun baked Jeff, and the smells around him rose like fumes from a rich, overripe vegetable soup. Sweet, pungent, rotten smells. He smelled fish in one nostril, and rotten fruit flowed through the other. The morning . . . the memory of the coolness of the predawn air was like a dream.

Danny said he was going out to the wreckers later to find a door for a VW he was working on. 'Can't see Tracy tonight, she's working late at the market.'

'You going to pick her up?'

'Can't, I've got to do some reading for my class. Bet Mr. Farah's going to flunk me again.'

Jeff stared up at the blue sky, and then he slept.

A banging on the side of the truck woke him. He opened his eyes and looked up into the trees. He saw the peaked roof of the Belco house elbowed into the blue sky and Mary's attic window, open now like a crooked eye. And then he saw her, looking out, the princess in the tower looking down at the prince disguised as a garbage collector.

6

Jeff had worked out the moment when he'd finally meet Mary – the Big Scene – ten different ways. He might be alone or it might happen with supporting actors. With Danny or Mrs. Belco or Danny's little brother, Robert. Even Muffin, one of the Belco cats, worked itself into his scenario.

JEFF: Hello.
MARY: Hello. And who is this?
JEFF: Jeff Orloff. And who is this? Little Mary Silver? And what has Little Mary Silver been up to?

Cut! Why the sarcasm? What was he afraid of? Another take.

JEFF (*sincere*): I've heard so much about you.

Cut! That was subject to misinterpretation, too. Once more.

JEFF (*surprised*): You here? I didn't even know you knew the Belcos.

Cut! That suggested he knew more about Mary than he cared to admit. Again.

JEFF (*simply*): Hi, nice to meet you. Are you here long? Visiting your family? Friends? Good, good. Nice time of the year to be up north. Get away from that southern heat. Yes, it gets hot here, but it isn't the same kind of heat . . .

When he first saw her, it was as if someone had grabbed him by the throat. She was sitting in the Belco kitchen on the couch, holding a doll. It was Mary, a Mary he didn't know, with bare legs and white ankle socks and this doll in her lap.

He reacted defensively. Struck a pose, hand on the wall. Steadying himself. Director Orloff's commanding presence escaped him. He froze, forgot his lines, forgot how to move, forgot where to stand. She looked at him without recognition. This was unbelievable. She used to smile at him. Had he changed that much? He was shaving every day now.

She looked old, but young. Young and old both. Ordinary and undistinguished. Two eyes, a bit of a nose, a line for a mouth. A cartoonist might have drawn it. A plain, ordinary face. Who'd stuck that baby in her lap?

The baby looked at him, too, round eyed and openly.

Mary? Baby? Who was she? What was he doing here? Where did he fit in? He didn't. He'd come over to see what she was like. Simple curiosity. Mary Silver was no friend of his. Just a girl he'd known in high school, a girl who could act, someone he'd admired from afar. Well, he'd seen her.

Leave, he told himself. And he would have left, but she was looking at him. Looking at him with those eyes, those large, extraordinary eyes, her expression apprehensive and worried.

She looked at him once, and then again, and he seemed to see her for the first time. See that plain face.

'Introduce yourself, Jeff.' Mrs. Belco was heating the baby's bottle. 'Where's your friend Daniel? I sent him to the store for a bag of potatoes an hour ago.' She tried a drop on her wrist, then handed it to Mary. 'Perfect. Jeff is a friend of Danny's.'

'Jeff Orloff,' he said, clicking his heels together, a moronic gesture. 'Orloff, like oarlock, one *l*, two *f*s.' Clever. He waited for the light of recognition, the mouth rounded, the eyes open wide. Jeff Orloff. Not *the* Jeff Orloff!

'Didn't you go to North?' she said.

He reached down to stroke Muffin. Didn't you go to North? Great powers of observation, Ms. Silver. Go to the head of the class. Did you go there, too? I never saw you, either.

'It was such a big school,' she said. Was she apologizing? 'I don't remember a lot of people.'

He rubbed Muffin's ears.

She glanced at him, then looked away, giving the same large-eyed attention to the refrigerator, the sink, the counters. He flung himself at the refrigerator, one arm over the top. Buddies. Good old refrigerator, and there were his pals, the toaster, the blender, and the popcorn machine. Our Gang.

His foot jiggled. He stepped on it. Then his finger started tapping. She was looking around. Was the Belco kitchen good enough for someone like Mary Silver? He hadn't missed the gold around her neck and the expensive-looking watch with the broad gold strap. She didn't fool him with this not knowing a lot of people in school bit. She knew the ones who counted, and he wasn't one of them.

He decided he didn't like her, not at all. Now that he saw her up close and they were talking – after a fashion – he wondered why he had ever been interested. Adolescent delusions. She wasn't pretty, not the way Tracy was. She didn't try to make herself attractive, either. Her hair was coarse and thick and she wore it like a mop, tied back loosely. Her eyes were her one good feature. Cool, beautiful eyes. She looked so bored with everything, glancing out the window, then picking a bit of lint off the baby.

His foot was hopping again. His feet wanted to go. Why didn't he follow? Why stand here, clinging to the refrigerator like a shipwrecked sailor? Leave. But he couldn't, just as he couldn't look at her and couldn't not look at her.

He slapped the side of the refrigerator with hearty familiarity. 'Mrs. B! What's there to eat around here?' He wasn't hungry.

'You know where the food is, Jeff. You're leaning on it.'

Mary glanced at Jeff. Was she remembering him from

the Drama Club now? Was she sorry he was there? Was this baby something she didn't want anyone to know about? Well, she'd sure come to the wrong place.

Just then Danny walked in. 'Where are my potatoes?' his mother said.

'What potatoes?'

'What potatoes! You were gone long enough. Forgot them? After I sent you for them special? Ten pounds of potatoes. I'll break your neck, Danny.'

Danny reached around behind him and produced the bag. 'I like to see you steam, Ma. I took Tracy home.'

'The minute you get near a girl you lose your brains. Sometimes I think you boys have your brains in your pants.'

Jeff glanced at Mary. She was fussing over the baby, smoothing its hair, then pressing her lips to its head.

Fade in: Proud Mary with baby, foul-mouthed mother-in-law and uncomfortable father standing nearby.

Cut! He had put himself into the picture. Was he the father? He could be the father . . . No, you couldn't. Yes, I could. If thoughts are father to the deed . . . If Mary pointed a finger at me and said, You are the one . . .

Fade in: A courtroom. Puritan Boston. JEFFREY *in the witness box.* COTTON MATHER *is the prosecutor. He wears a dark suit with a wide white collar.*

Q: Jeff Orloff, answer yes or no. Do you know the plaintiff?

A: Know, sire?

Q: You deny knowing her?

A: No, sire, but not that way.

Q: What way? You knew her! (*The prosecutor hammers the table with his fist.*) You knew her.

A: Yes, sire.

Q: You made a portrait of the plaintiff that you stared at hungrily. You had many of these portraits on your wall.

A: Yes, sire.

Q: And when you regarded these portraits you had unlawful, lewd, and lascivious thoughts about the plaintiff?

A: Yes, sire.

Q: On many occasions. How many? Speak up, boy, this is a court of law.

A: Many, sire.

Q: Carnal thoughts of copulation? Sit up, boy, don't sink under the seat. Show some backbone. Own up to it like a man.

A: Yes, sire.

Q: Carnal thoughts?

A: Yes, sire.

Q: Thoughts of copulation?

A: Yes, sire.

Q: And the innocent babe, did you consider it?

A: No, sire.

Q: It was nothing to you, a doll, something to be tossed aside.

A: Yes, sire.

Q: Guilty on all counts!

DAME BELCO (*rises to her feet*): Brains in his pants! Brains in his pants!

'Jeff . . .'

'Ahh . . .'

'Jeff . . . Jeff!'

His head came up. 'Yes, sire!'

Mrs. Belco stood back, looking at him. 'We love Jeff, he's so funny sometimes.'

But the way Mary looked at him, if that's what you could call it, she didn't think he was that funny. She didn't think he was funny at all. What had he said or done, but grunt. That's the way she was looking at him, like someone who grunted a lot.

7

Jeff, barefooted, barechested, and spattered with paint, stood on the ground squinting up at the wall. His hands were sticky, and there was a crick in his shoulder. The fresh paint was dazzling, iridescent, like a falling sheet of white peacock's feathers. Above him Mary appeared in a pure white gown, shimmering on the wall, out of reach but smiling down at him like the painted Virgin in the Cathedral. He reached his hand out to her. Mary, untouched, filled with perfect knowledge.

Oh, really?

The purity of his dream had been sullied, stained. He stood staring at the wall, his nose jammed against the clapboards. You're a fool. Paint, fool. And he slapped the paint on in great gobs and then worked like a fury spreading it before it all dripped on the ground.

He was quitting, just coming down the ladder, when Danny appeared, driving his VW van. 'I need you, Jeff.' He was wearing his Green Sentry baseball uniform. 'I'm pitching tonight. We're playing the top team in the league, McCulloch's Tavern, and you're going to cheer our side.'

Jeff hopped off the ladder. 'Wait till I clean up.' Ten minutes later, his head wet and wearing a clean shirt, he came running out, packing his camera and some extra film in a shoulder bag. Some important footage was going to be shot tonight. He'd been thinking about doing a baseball film. Something quintessential, that went straight to the heart of the game.

'We're picking up Tracy first,' Danny said.

'More support.'

'Right. I thought we'd do something afterward.'

'I'm invited to that, too?'

'I just said you were. It's more fun when there's a crowd.'

'I'm a crowd.'

'That's the idea.'

'If you invited Mary Silver, there'd be four of us.'

'Why her?'

Jeff eyed a row of passing houses through the camera. 'I don't know, she might like to do something.'

'She doesn't like to do anything.'

'How do you know that?'

'I live in the same house with her, don't I? She doesn't do anything. Just sits up in her room with her baby and reads.'

Jeff put his feet up on the dashboard.

Danny reached over and knocked his feet down. 'What are you, still interested in her? If you want my advice—'

'I don't.' He didn't want to hear a lot of pious drivel about Mary. 'Belco, why don't you look where you're driving?' And he put his feet back up on the dashboard.

Truman Park was a big scruffy dry field at the edge of South Bay Road. A couple of baseball diamonds, a scattering of cars behind home plate, and people sitting in folding lawn chairs, with their kids running around. Somebody had a stereo set up and going full blast.

Jeff and Tracy sprawled out on the grass by first base. That is, he sprawled while Tracy, in a pair of tight shorts, posed with one leg outstreched, knee raised. As the Green Sentries took the field, she cupped her hands. 'Go get 'em, Danny!'

Jeff focused the camera and took a shot of her. He couldn't take his eyes off the inside of her creamy smooth thighs. Tracy prodded him. 'How about giving Danny a cheer?'

'Go, Danny!' He swung the camera and caught Danny on the mound wiping his forehead. The knees were torn out of his green playing pants. He pulled his cap down, squinted at the batter. There was a man on first and no outs. The Green Sentries were already behind 3–0. 'Keep it low!' the third baseman yelled.

Flat on his belly, Jeff panned the camera low across the field. There was something about this field, something about people coming together to play and to watch . . . It was happening everywhere. If he could get up high enough, he'd see people playing baseball all over America in scruffy fields like this one, full of dust and faded grass. In back of high schools and in empty city lots and playgrounds and in the streets. And in Truman Parks and Kennedy Parks and Eisenhower Parks, in towns like Phoenix and Waterville and Central Square.

He swung the camera around on Tracy again. 'How'd you like to be in a major motion picture?'

'Little me?' She sat back and pushed out her chest. Across her yellow T-shirt in black letters it said, HANDS OFF.

'You'll be the star. It's a baseball movie.'

'Then I want to play centre field.'

'No, you can't. You're going to be the hero's girlfriend.'

She tossed her chin up and fluffed her hair. 'Why can't I be his girlfriend and play centre field?'

'Because they don't make movies that way.'

'Why not? If I'm the star, I want to be the centre fielder.'

'The director says no. In this movie you like two guys. The hero and his best friend.'

Tracy dusted off her shirt. 'That's interesting. That I like.'

'I thought you would.'

Tracy studied her legs. 'What part are you going to take? The best friend or the boyfriend?'

'Told you, I'm the director.'

'Too bad. You'd be a cute boyfriend.'

'So, do we sign a contract? I'd like to get your commitment for this project in writing.'

'What's my cut?'

'Cut! I thought you were doing it for love and friendship.' He found a stick and scratched a mark in the dust. 'Sign here,' he said. 'I'm flying to the coast tonight. Shooting starts in ten days.'

'Sorry, but I have a full schedule. I'm working and taking a class.'

'Oh, Tracy, what did you flunk?'

'Nothing,' she said indignantly, and tossed her head. Tracy was an expert on those girl-girl things. 'I'm taking a modelling seminar this summer, that's my class.'

'Really, what are you going to learn?' He ran a blade of grass over her leg. 'How to paint your toenails?'

Tracy glanced over as the other team took the field. 'I'm learning how to stand and walk and how to wear clothes properly.'

'You still don't know that?'

She kicked him. 'Fun-ny. I'm learning how to model so I can enter the county beauty pageant.'

'You think you're going to win?'

'Don't you?'

'I think you can do anything you want to do.'

'Do you mean it?'

'Sure, I mean it. I'd vote for you.'

'I can never tell if you're serious or not.'

'I'm being one hundred percent serious. You could be Miss America if you wanted to enough.' He sat up. 'You believe that?'

She pushed him back. 'I'm not crazy.'

He let himself fall over backward and she sat on him, her knees on his shoulders. Whoom. The blood went crashing through him.

'What's that look in your eye?'

'What look? It's the setting sun.'

She put her hand over his eyes. 'I'm going to shut those hot eyes of yours.'

He grabbed her wrist.

She broke free. 'Danny's watching us . . . Play ball,' she yelled, then she clapped her hands. 'Go get them, Danny, pitch them out of there.'

Danny adjusted his cap and spit in the dirt. Then he threw three straight pitches right over the batter's head.

Jeff and Tracy behaved themselves after that, but the damage was done. After the game Danny wouldn't talk to either of them.

'Great game,' Jeff said. Danny was pulling off his cleats while Tracy massaged his back. 'You really pitched a good one.'

'How do you know? You weren't watching.'

Then the van wouldn't start, and he kicked it in the tyre. The battery was dead, and they had to push. That is, Jeff and Tracy pushed while Danny sat in the driver's seat and gave the orders. 'Push! Push, you slobs. Harder!' Tracy kicked off her high-heeled sandals. They pushed the van all the way up to the road. And then off Danny went.

'There he goes,' Jeff said. The sweat was running down his cheeks. He sank down next to Tracy.

'Look at my nails,' she said. 'That Danny, he's so damn jealous. No sense of humour.'

But when Danny came back for them, he was smiling. 'You two sure are in lousy shape,' he said.

8

Sunday was hot and overcast. It was barbecue day in the neighbourhood. A pall of charcoal lighter and steak fumes hung in the air. The Orloffs, too, were out in back on their terrace. Barbecued steak was his father's speciality. Everyone was talking about meat. 'How do you want your steak, Donna?'

'Make hers medium,' Jeff's brother said, 'and mine rare.'

'Jeff, how do you want your meat?'

'No meat.' Jeff closed his eyes and tried not to breathe the grease in the air. He thought about Mary, got a little heat in his stomach. *Cut!* He wasn't interested. She wasn't interested. Think about what you're going to do. Assume Hollywood. When do you go? How do you get there? Who's going to hire you? *Cut!* That was his father's line.

He rolled over in the grass and lay with his mouth on his arm. Sniffed his arm. Paint, kerosene, grass. He bit himself. Salty. He kissed his arm, imagining that it was her arm.

Was he in love? Something stupid like that. Maybe he was a little bit obsessed. A little obsessed? Was there such a thing as a mild obsession? Not for him. Always obsessed – that was the story of his life.

'Is he still flaked out?' he heard his brother say. 'Hey, Jeffo, wake up.' His brother squatted down next to him. 'You still asleep?'

Something seared Jeff's skin – hot coals or a branding iron. His playful brother had just branded him with an icy can of beer on his bare back. He sprang up. 'I can see why your patients get cured, Dr. Orloff. They're just glad to get away from you.'

Jules was a psychologist at Henninger Institute. Dr. Orloff. Balding and overweight, he looked like an Indian

Buddha. 'That was a dirty trick, wasn't it?' he said cheerfully, putting his arm around Jeff. 'I thought of giving you a hotfoot, but I couldn't bring myself to do it on your bare feet.'

'You're all heart.' Jeff sat down next to Donna. 'Donna, do you see what kind of man you married? A sadist.'

He liked his sister-in-law. She was tall and fair, a botanist who taught at Community College, the only quiet one in the family and the only one in the family as interested in movies as he was. 'What did you think of the remake of *Mutiny on the Bounty?*' Jeff said.

'I thought it was exciting.'

'A sincere effort. Did you like the scene in the lifeboat?'

'Yes!'

'I thought they were pushing my buttons.'

He was just warming to the subject when the phone rang. 'Get that, Jeff,' his mother said.

'I'm talking.'

'It's for you.'

'How do you know that,' he said as he headed for the phone. 'Hello.' It was his sister, Natalie.

'Hey, Natalie! Natalie, my favourite sister.'

'I finally got you, Jeff. You're a hard man to get hold of. Mom says she never knows where you are half the time. I want to warn you,' she said, 'I'm going to talk about college. I promised Dad I'd pitch to you.'

Did he really want to hear this? 'Let's change the subject, Natalie.' When he thought about growing up, it was Natalie he remembered. She was the one who took care of him while his mother worked, the one he ran to when he hurt or needed help, or just had to talk to someone.

'I haven't said anything yet. What I was going to say is that college is a reasonable place for you to be at this time. Don't say anything. I'm not through. It's a good place to think. Learn. Grow. Find out about yourself. I don't want to hassle you. But think about it. Next topic, are you coming to my wedding, or not?'

'I don't know.' He told his parents he'd fly down and back the same day. He'd even offered to pay. But his father had exploded. 'Spend that money when the car's right there!' It was hard for him to say no to his sister, but even for her, he couldn't see spending all that time in close quarters with his father. He'd either disagree with everything his father said or go into a funk and not talk the whole week.

'Give me a straight answer, yes or no.'

'First of all, I'd ruin things for Mom and Dad. That would make them so miserable they'd make me miserable and then I'll be mean and miserable to everyone else and spoil your wedding. Besides, I've got a job. I'm saving money.'

'For college?'

'That's the second time you've used that word.'

'I can't get you to change your mind?'

'About college or coming to the wedding? Are you really going to be upset if I don't come?'

'We'll survive. Listen, Jeff, actually the wedding isn't that big a deal. We've been living together for almost three years now.'

His future brother-in-law was a veterinarian with a successful suburban practice, a man of achievements and accomplishments. Men of achievement made Jeff bristle. Or was he just jealous?

'Sure we can't help you change your mind about the wedding?'

'No way. I'd like to, but there's a lot going on in my life.' Again, like a shooting star, Mary's name raced through his mind. What was she doing right this second? Had his name just flashed through her mind? Fat chance.

Afterward, Jeff went outside again. 'I left your steak on the coals,' his father said. He had difficulty remembering that Jeff didn't eat meat. Jeff sat down at the edge of the table next to Donna and picked up a celery stalk.

'Did you talk to David?' Donna said.

'I hear you were accepted at three colleges,' his brother said. 'Which one is it going to be?'

So, this was the highlight of the picnic. This was Get Jeff on the Right Track Day. First his sister. Now it was Jules' and Donna's turn. 'I'm still thinking about it,' he said.

'You're going to think yourself right out of school.'

'Is that the official Orloff opinion?'

'Are you feeling harassed?' Jules said professionally.

'You bet your doctor's ass. What have you guys been doing, running a hotline down to Washington? What am I, the family entertainment?'

'Why are you acting this way?' his brother said.

'Are you charging me for this, Doctor?'

'You're tense.'

Jeff bared his teeth.

'You're raising your voice, you're swearing.'

'Goddammit, I'm not swearing.'

His brother smiled. 'We all went through this rebellious stage. It's pretty routine. You think you can speed things up a little?'

'Okay. Let's speed things up. I'm leaving for California tomorrow morning. Nothing else to discuss. I'm not asking you guys for money.' He made his points with the celery stalk. 'I've been working. Saving my money. How will I get out there? Maybe I'll hitchhike. No? Too much anxiety? I'll take a bus. How will I live? Get a job. What kind of job? A menial job. Any other questions? I'll be happy to answer. Dad, you want to know how many directors earn a living at it. Answer? Always room for one more. Ah, Mom, you want to know if they're waiting for me with open arms. Answer? That stumps me.'

'A-hah . . .' his brother said.

'A-hah, what?'

His brother leaned on his elbow. 'A-hah means go on.'

'Is that what they taught you in adolescent psych?'

'A-hah.'

His mother took his hand. 'Jeff. Slow down. I know you're angry that we—'

'Mom! Are you turning psychologist, too?'

'Don't you know everything costs double in California?' his father said. He of the dashing moustache and worried face. He started giving Jeff the Economics Is Life argument. 'Without money, you can't get anywhere. And nobody gives it away.'

Jeff slumped. Money! Money! Money! Money, savings accounts – that was his parents' life. For them, money was like food. They stored it and it gave them a full, satisfied feeling. They had money in different banks and they stored money in the house, especially in the kitchen, in the teapot and in the freezer. Their happiest moments were when they were talking to each other about money.

'You think that going to college and directing contradict each other?' his father said.

'As far as I'm concerned, yes.'

'You're dreaming. I used to dream, too. And then I grew up. There's a real world out there, and it isn't what you dream it is. You don't get what you want in this world. Nobody does. You have to get into the jammed elevators and smell the folks. You have to sit in a polluted factory when you'd rather be out fishing. But that's life. That's what ninety-nine and nine-tenths percent of the folks have to do.'

Jeff felt his father's words beating down on him. He looked at his hands. They were all looking down, and now nobody seemed to have anything to say. When his father came out with this stuff, it depressed everyone. It was the same defeated, crappy view of life he had always had. Had his father really ever dreamed? Jeff couldn't believe it.

9

It was raining, a warm rain, when Jeff went over to the Belcos'. His hair was wet and his shirt, too. In the house, the lights were on. Mary was in the front hall, surrounded by boxes. 'Moving in?'

'Oh, hi,' she said. She picked up a box and started up the stairs.

'Want some help?'

'No, thanks.'

Hands in his pockets, jiggling change, Jeff wandered into the kitchen, then stepped out in the hall again when he heard Mary coming back down. 'Glad to help. I'm not doing anything but hanging around.'

She hesitated, looked at him closely, frowned at him. This was a big decision.

'I don't charge that much,' he said.

That got him a smile, at least the beginnings of one. But no purchase orders.

'I can manage.'

In the kitchen Danny was bent over, concentrating on the newspaper, lipreading, running his finger down the page. Mrs. Belco brushed Jeff aside. 'Sit down or get out of the way. Danny, get your brother some milk.'

Danny got the milk, then stood by the refrigerator reading the paper. His mother grabbed the container and poured Robert's milk. 'Sit down, Jeff, join the party. The menu today is hot tomato soup and grilled cheese sandwiches.'

'Mom, how many balls of twine does it take to get to the moon?' Robert said.

She dropped a grilled cheese sandwich in front of him. 'I give up. Danny, put the paper down.'

'The answer,' Robert said, 'is one ball of twine, but it's *real* big.'

'Danny! Are you going to eat your lunch? What time are you supposed to be in school?'

'Mom, will you slow down.'

'Slow down? Who's going to let me? Maybe when I die.'

Danny handed Jeff the folded sports section and pointed to the baseball results. 'Look whose name is in the paper.'

'Let me see, Jeff.' Mrs. Belco bent over the paper. 'You're famous, my son.'

'Yeah, Ma.' Danny clasped his hands over his head.

Mrs. Belco poured tea into a brown teapot, then put it on a tray with a sandwich. 'You boys want anything else, you take care of yourselves. I'm taking this tray up to Mrs. Brown and then I'm taking my rest.' She left. A moment later, there was a crash in the hall. 'Danny,' Mrs. Belco yelled. 'Jeff! Help Mary get these boxes out of here before somebody kills themselves.'

'Can't,' Danny yelled back. 'I'm late already.'

'I'll do it,' Jeff said, going out.

Mary was on her way up with another box. Jeff grabbed a box and hurried after her. 'What have you got in here, rocks?' Silence. Not that he gave a damn. Charming Ms. Silver was breathing hard. He went up the stairs, whistling. Notice, I'm not even winded.

In her room he looked around curiously. 'Where do you want this?'

She pointed to a wall.

It was a small attic room with a sloping ceiling and two square recessed windows. Rain drummed on the roof. Tight little room – bed, two bureaus jammed together, a crib against one wall, a hi-fi on the floor, a pink tub full of baby toys, and the baby herself in a walker in the middle of the room.

'Hello, baby,' Jeff said.

'Her name is Hannah.'

47

'Cozy room you've got.'

'It's a mess.'

'You should see mine. And I've been living in it for eighteen years.'

She frowned at the room. Frowned. Frowned at him, frowned at everything. Hannah wheeled toward him. The kid was more interested in him than Mary was. 'Thanks for the help,' she said, dismissing him.

'I'm not done yet. I've got my orders from General Belco.' He went down again for another load. On the way up, she passed him going down. 'We'll get this done in no time,' he said. He was cheerful, he was friendly, he was helpful. He was a jerk. She must think he was a Boy Scout working on his Good Neighbour badge.

'You could work on your room while I bring up the rest of the stuff,' he said.

'Look, if I need advice I'll ask for it.'

'Oops, wrong door.' He went flying down the stairs again, the sound of his feet covering up his chagrin. Keep your mouth shut, Orloff! He brought the remaining boxes up in silence.

As he brought up the last box, he passed Mary standing outside Mrs. Belco's room, talking to her through the door. 'Is anybody going downtown later?' he heard Mary say. The baby was in her arms. 'Hannah has a doctor appointment and I don't want to take her out in the rain.'

'I can't help you,' Mrs. Belco said. 'I've got to get some sleep. Maybe you ought to call a cab. Why didn't you ask Danny when he was here?'

Jeff stacked the last box. When he went downstairs, Mary was going through the phone book. 'That's it,' he said. 'Everything's upstairs.'

'Thanks,' Mary said. She hesitated. 'Yeah . . . yes, thanks a lot.' She stuck out her hand.

'No problem.' They were holding hands. Sort of. He

was grateful. He was inordinately grateful. Grateful beyond reason. 'Listen,' he said. 'I'll take you to the doctor's.'

'You? Do you have a car?'

'Sure.' He'd have to get the car from Danny.

'I'll pay you.'

'I didn't say anything about money. Just tell me what time.'

She looked at her watch. 'I have to leave in an hour.'

'I'll be here.'

He ran from the Belco house to North High. Danny was in class already. It was a small class, maybe twelve kids. The teacher, Mr. Farah, was a friend of Jeff's from Drama Club days. He was reading to the class. Everyone was sprawled out, looking half asleep.

Jeff greeted Mr. Farah. 'Is it okay? I just want to talk to Danny for a minute.'

Mr. Farah came to the door. He was nearly bald, and to compensate he let his hair grow long in back. 'How are you doing, Jeff?' Even after Jeff left Drama Club, they'd spent a lot of hours talking. 'You setting the world on its ear?'

'Washing dishes at Sadie's Diner. Does that qualify? How about painting my family's house?'

'So you haven't made up your mind about college yet? That's okay. Just remember, whatever you do, I expect a lot from you.' He motioned to Danny. 'Five minutes.'

When they were alone, Danny said, 'What do you want? What's the heat?'

'The keys.' Jeff put out his hand.

'Where are you going?'

'Just give me the keys, Belco.' He started going through Danny's pockets.

Danny knocked his hands away. 'What do you want them for?'

'I'm giving Mary Silver a ride to the doctor's.'

Danny held him off. 'Mary? Did she ask you?'

49

'Sort of. Come on, hand them over.'

A smile slowly spread across Danny's broad face.

'Don't look so smug,' Jeff said. 'It's not what you think.'

10

Driving Mary to the doctor, he talked and talked. The flood gates were open. Mary was sitting inches from him with the baby wired up in a chest harness. She looked like a parachutist getting ready to bail out over enemy territory. And that made his tongue flap twice as fast.

'This is my first summer out of school,' he said. 'Post school, you might say, postmortem . . . In school we die and then . . .' He gestured. 'How do you like this town? You got away, but I'm still serving time. It's so bad. There's nothing in this town. Now that's the one positive thing about it. It's so bad, and it's going to feel so good to get away. That's how I'm going to remember this town. As my launchpad.'

The launchpad image was an unfortunate one. Excessive. He was trying too hard. It made him sound pompous. 'I'm like a frog in a mudhole. What I can't decide is which way to jump. Hollywood or New York? They're the only two places to go if you're going to be a director. I'm leaning towards Hollywood at the moment. What do you think?'

He paused democratically. He wasn't hogging the conversation. Agree, disagree, give your opinion. Anything. Class, there will be a quiz at the end of this lecture. You will be judged on memory and comprehension.

Her silence made him nervous. She was sitting next to him, but where was she? In Argentina? China? Home in bed? For an actress she didn't project much. Totally self-absorbed.

Well, he was pretty self-absorbed himself. He wanted to get through to her. Had to. When was he going to get a chance like this again? He wanted her to know him. (Modest Jeff Orloff.) How could she tell what he was really like inside, behind the cage of bone where his heart lay, when every time he started talking, what came out was this mad, jittery flood of words.

'What I have been doing this summer is getting my shit together, if you get my drift.' He glanced at her. Keep talking, Orloff, and she's going to roll the window down at the next intersection and scream for help.

She pressed her lips to Hannah's forehead. 'I think she might have a fever. She wouldn't eat this morning, and she was cranky all day yesterday.'

The kid looked all right to him. 'I don't know that much about babies,' he admitted, and went back to talking about himself. 'My family doesn't understand anything I want to do.'

'Families are all alike.' She wiped Hannah's mouth.

'Not your family.' Her family, he imagined, was the opposite of his. The Silvers appreciated the artistic. There would be music in their house and paintings on the wall, and they'd be proud of their daughter, supporting and encouraging her. They'd have a whole room given to pictures of Mary in the different roles she'd played.

'What's your next step? Is your family going to help you pursue your career?' Pursue your career. *Cut!* Why couldn't he say what he meant without sounding like he was running for office?

'What career?'

'Acting.'

'I'm not an actress.'

'You are. I saw you act in school. You were the best. I never forgot it. Even then you were a lot more than just a student actress.'

'Thanks for the kind words, but you're wrong. I am not an actress,' she said emphatically. 'I haven't done anything, I'm not likely to do anything, and I really don't want to talk about it.' She twisted her hair up and held it on top of her head.

Even that little motion was exciting, actorish. How could she not know that she was an actress?

She was looking out the window again. Subject closed. Her face said, I talk about myself to people I like. Not to people I'm indifferent to.

The rest of the way to Irving Avenue, he clammed up and concentrated on his driving.

When she came out of the doctor's office, she was a changed person. She was smiling at him. 'The doctor says Hannah's teething. Can you imagine, it's that simple and I thought it was something awful I did. That's why she's cranky, and she does have a little fever. He wants me to get a thermometer and baby aspirin. Could we stop at a drugstore on the way back?'

When they left the drugstore, it was still raining. They ducked into the Baskin-Robbins next door, bought ice cream cones, and ate them in the car. He accepted a cone in the interests of good fellowship. He didn't want to break the mood and tell her about all the chemical junk used in ice cream.

She started talking about the baby again and her fever and her teeth. The subject bored him, but Mary's eyes were wonderful. He couldn't stop looking at her and almost drove into a parked car.

'Watch it!' she said.

'Sorry. I saw it.'

'Maybe I'm talking too much. I'm distracting you.'

Oh, that was true. He gave her an understanding look. 'Sometimes you have to talk. It can't be easy to be alone.'

'You don't know how hard it is until it happens to you. Have you ever been alone?'

'Not exactly – but you can be alone even if there are a lot of people around.'

She nodded. 'That's true, too.'

The minute she got friendly he got horny. Sex hadn't

53

even been on his mind. It was automatic, something that happened to him with girls anywhere. But cars and girls in combination, especially girls he liked, that was dynamite. He was having trouble keeping the damned thing decent and his foot on the gas at the same time. He was a traffic hazard. If a cop stopped him now, he was going to get a ticket for an unlawful erection.

Hannah leaned towards him, got her wet hands on his face.

'I don't think you like me, you little slob.'

Mary wiped the baby's mouth with her fingers. 'You know, she doesn't talk, but she understands everything.'

'Hannah, I apologize. You're not a slob, just a little sloppy.' When he looked at Hannah, she was watching him.

'She likes men,' Mary said.

'Then it's no compliment to me.'

'You want her just to like you?'

He gave Mary an intent look. 'Not very realistic, am I?'

When they got back to the Belcos', Mary tried to give him some money. 'Don't insult me.'

'I'd like to pay you.'

'Just put it down to friendship.'

'You hardly know me.' She finally put the money away. 'I really appreciate it, Jeff.'

It didn't escape him that she'd used his name for the first time. 'Anytime you need a ride or anything, Mary, any kind of help . . . think of me.' He racked his brain for a way to keep her in the car. It's been nice . . . Can we do this again . . . When am I going to see you? But finally he just sat there and watched her walk away.

Parting sequence (freeze shot): Mary caught as she goes up the steps of the house (*underneath, violins soar*).

11

After the bright August heat outside, the cool, air-conditioned darkness of the movie house was like a balm to Jeff's skin. There was excitement in the air, a smell of anticipation, of popcorn and chocolate. His father thought going to a movie in the middle of the day was degenerate and un-American, in the same category as bedwetting and kinky sex, but Jeff liked nothing better. He went all the way down front, where he took the catbird seat, centre aisle, the director's seat.

Previews were being shown as he sat down. Here and there up front were other singles, nuts like himself who liked to get their heads right into the screen. He'd seen this film five times before, but there were so many things he missed on the first viewing, the second, the third, even the fifth.

Behind him he heard a baby shrieking, and he twisted around. A few days ago the sound would have been meaningless, but now he scooted back and found Mary and Hannah sitting on the side aisle. Even in the dark he recognized Mary.

'Hey,' he whispered, sliding into the seat next to her, 'I didn't know you liked the movies.'

'Where'd you come from?' she said. There was a box of popcorn in her lap.

'I practically live here. I'm a fanatic. I've seen this picture five times.'

'Is it that good?'

'The photography is incredible.'

Hannah moved around in Mary's arms. 'Shh!' Mary said, rescuing the popcorn. 'You have to be quiet, sugar.'

'Here, let me hold that.' He took the popcorn and turned so he was facing Mary, his arm behind her seat. 'You're going to love this picture,' he said as the movie began. 'Look at those long flat establishing shots, look at the way the director got the feeling of that Texas landscape.'

'Please. I want to watch.'

Of course he was talking too much. Again. But he couldn't help himself. Here he was in the movies, watching one of his favourite films with Mary Silver. He tapped her shoulder. 'We'll talk afterward.' Nervously, he picked at the popcorn, going through half the box before he caught himself. He didn't even like it. 'You better take this,' he said, handing it back to her. 'I'll go get you some more.'

She shook her head. She didn't seem to be as thrilled about him talking as he was. He tried to watch silently, but a moment later he was at it again. 'Do you see how carefully he put the movie together? Not a wasted motion. Every movement tells the story.'

Mary kept her eyes fixed on the screen.

'This is the last thing I'm going to say. That's a fifties motel. You see how the units were all separate? And you see that light outside each unit? Now, that's perfect.'

Behind, someone hissed. Pests. People were always complaining. He noticed a really strong smell in the air and nudged Mary. He waved his hand in front of his nose. Mary suddenly got to her feet, and clutching Hannah, brushed past him. It took him a moment to catch on, and then he followed her.

She wasn't in the lobby. The girl at the candy counter told him a woman and a baby had just gone into the bathroom. He waited by the water fountain.

When Mary came out, she looked upset. He thought she was worried about missing part of the movie. 'Listen, I can fill you in, word for word. And if you want to, we can see it through from the beginning again. It's better the second time, anyway.'

That's when she walked out of the theatre.

'Where you going?' He followed her out.

She put Hannah into the shoulder carrier. 'Are you always like this?' She blew out her breath. 'Look, maybe, I'm a little upset. Things upset me—' She stopped. 'What am I saying? I don't have to apologize to you. I just want to be left alone. Okay?'

'Okay,' he said. 'I respect that. Maybe next time,' he added hopefully.

'Next time what?'

'Next time we see each other. Next time we get together—'

'We're getting together? Where'd you get that idea? Look, you helped me out the other day and I appreciate it, but that's it. I don't know what you're thinking, but leave me out of it.'

She was determined to be unfriendly and he was just as determined to be friendly. 'You'd make me feel a lot better if you went back and saw the rest of the movie.'

'You really are incredible.'

'No, seriously – I have the guilts.'

'That's your problem.'

Things hadn't gotten off exactly on the right foot, but he wasn't discouraged. 'You want me to carry Hannah?' he said.

She looked up to the sky. A silent prayer. *Why am I chosen?*

Didn't she really know? 'Sometimes you feel so good around somebody you forget where you are and you think everything you feel she's feeling. Don't you have those great feelings sometimes, like you're on the threshold of something great? I mean life, don't you love it?' He couldn't believe the things he was saying. Somebody, put a lock on my mouth.

'I used to have stars in my eyes, too. No more.'

'What happened?'

'Come on, don't be stupid.'

She finally got him. 'Listen, am I bugging you? Say the word and I'll split.'

'Too bad you didn't think of that sooner.' She looked down the street for a bus. 'Do you act this way with every girl you meet? Move in on her?'

He put his hands in his pockets and backed off. 'Sorry. I guess I just assumed too much.'

She looked for the bus again. 'Don't these buses ever come around here?'

He pointed in the direction the Belcos lived. 'It's not that far to Spring Street. It's over there.'

'I know where they live.' Everything he said seemed to irritate her. She started walking and he walked along, not quite behind her but not with her, either. He *had* moved in on her. He could apologize. But hadn't he apologized once? Or had he? If he hadn't, he should have. But if he had, another apology would only make things worse. He came up alongside her and tried again.

'How's that backpack? Is the baby heavy?'

She shook her head. 'I'm used to it.'

'It would be nice if she walked.'

'That's coming,' Mary said.

He picked a dandelion from the side of the road and stuck it in his shirt. 'When I was a kid, my father paid me half a cent for every dandelion I pulled out of the lawn.'

'I used to make crowns of dandelions from our front lawn,' she said.

'Want some?' He picked a handful. He wasn't sure she'd take them, but she did and started weaving them together.

'Give me longer stems,' she said. They walked along. When she was done she let Jeff put the crown on Hannah's head.

Hannah grabbed the crown and stuffed it in her mouth. 'She's impossible,' Mary said.

'That makes two of us,' he said.

'Tell me about it!' she said, but she was smiling.

12

Saturday morning, Jeff was painting when his father stuck his head out the door and told him there was a phone call for him. 'It's a girl.'

It was Mary. That was a surprise. Mary, on the phone and uncomfortable. 'Am I taking you away from something?'

'No.' He picked at a dry gob of paint on his shorts. 'Nothing I don't want to be taken away from.'

'You're not going to believe this. I apologize – I really don't think of you as an ambulance service, but I have a terrible toothache and the dentist said he'll see me if I come right down. Any chance of you driving me?'

'I don't have a car.'

'Oh!' A pause. 'That wasn't your car? I thought it was yours.'

'It was Danny's.'

'Oh. Well – I'll just have to figure something else out.'

'No, wait a minute. Hang on. Maybe I can get a car.'

His father was out in back, breaking off the faded flowers. 'Dad – how would you like to lend me your car for a while?'

'You're through painting?'

'I'll be back in a couple of hours, I promise.' Jeff checked his watch as proof of his sincerity. 'It's ten now. I'll be back at noon.'

His father twisted the ends of his moustache. 'Noontime.' He tossed Jeff the keys.

'Guaranteed. Thanks, Dad.'

Mary was waiting on the porch steps, holding Hannah in her arms, her free hand to her jaw. 'I can't smile,' she said, 'but I really, really appreciate this.' There was a vulnerable look to her. In her shorts and a shirt with the sleeves cut out, she looked like a kid babysitting Hannah.

On the way over, she didn't say much. Once she said did he mind coming in with her to watch Hannah? 'Don't say yes if you're busy. You could just leave me.'

'No, that's okay.'

In the dentist's office, she gave him Hannah and showed him the bottle of juice in the nappy bag. 'She likes to look at books.' She handed him a cloth book.

He held Hannah gingerly in his lap. She kept looking around at him. 'Whatever you're thinking of, Hannah, don't do it. Save it till your mother comes out.'

Her mouth took on a long, sad curve.

'Listen, don't turn on the waterworks, 'cause I'm more scared of you than you are of me.' He showed her the bottle. 'You want to drink?'

She grabbed the bottle, sucked on it for a moment, then threw it on the floor. He tried to put it back in her mouth. She spit it out. 'Come on,' he said, 'don't be like that. I'm not so bad, am I?' She considered it. 'I like little kids,' he continued, pleading his case. 'Ask Danny's little brother, Robert. He likes me.'

She listened, but when he tried to lean her against his arm and give her the bottle, she let out a sudden shriek. 'Hannah!' He put his fingers in his ears. 'You almost made me deaf.'

She shrieked again, then looked at him. Okay, it was a game now. 'Good try, but no prizes. Cut it out, or Mary's going to think I did something to you.'

She wriggled like a caterpillar and slid off his lap onto the floor. He caught her, and she giggled and toppled over again.

'So you want to play?' He sat down on the floor with her. She crawled away. He grabbed her foot. She protested, and he let her go. She scooted around the room, then stopped near the door to look over her shoulder to see what he was going to do.

When Mary came out, he was sitting on the floor, back to the door. Hannah was reading her book upside down. 'Were you good for Jeff?' Mary kissed Hannah on the mouth. 'Were you a good girl? How was she, Jeff?'

'No trouble. Easy as pie, she really was.'

Mary's jaw was numb. 'This is going to feel awful when the novocaine wears off,' she said in the car. 'The dentist said it was a really deep cavity, right next to the nerve.'

'I hate dentists,' he said.

'Everybody hates dentists.'

At the Belcos' she asked Jeff to carry Hannah upstairs. 'I'm feeling woozy.' She looked pale and he started to put his arm around her, but he stopped himself, remembering the way she reacted in the movie when he moved in on her. Well, that was her version. He didn't think he'd moved in on her.

Upstairs in her room, Mary put Hannah down for a nap, then stood there, rocking the crib. Jeff was uncertain if she wanted him to stay or go. The room looked unchanged – the same clutter, open boxes on the floor and clothes everywhere.

'Oh, my God.' Mary put her hand to her cheek. 'I can feel it throbbing. I need aspirin.' She began rummaging around on the top of the bureau next to the crib. 'There was some baby aspirin here. It's somewhere in this mess.' Hannah raised her head. 'Lie down, sugar, Mummy's got a toothache. Here—' She grabbed Jeff's hand. 'Rock her while I go downstairs and ask for some aspirin.' She ran out.

He rocked the crib. Hannah lay with her finger in her mouth, watching him. 'Tell me, kid—' He bent over the crib. 'Does she like me? Or am I just useful? You think she's liking me a little? I think so, too.'

Hannah was asleep when Mary returned. She held up a

bottle of aspirin. 'My fix,' she whispered. 'Mrs. Brown gave it to me.'

'Mrs. Century,' he whispered back.

'I said I'd go down and visit her after Hannah had her nap.'

'So you're all set—' He leaned toward the door.

'Wait, Jeff.' He thought she was going to offer to pay him. Instinctively he put his hands up. 'What's the matter?' she said. 'I just want to tell you, you saved my life today. And you helped me the other day. I don't know how to thank you.'

He sat down on the edge of the bed.

She walked around, moving her arms. 'That aspirin must be taking effect,' she said. 'I really feel better. Last night I was in so much pain I almost called my mother.' She sat down next to him and they talked in low tones.

'You had that toothache since last night?'

'I don't know how I got through the night.' She started rummaging through an open box. 'You don't want to hear about that.'

'Is that your mother?' He pointed to a framed colour photo of a heavyset woman standing in front of a palm tree.

'Yes.' Mary handed him the picture and took another one from the box. 'And here's my father.'

'They're in Florida?'

She touched the edge of her mouth. 'I'm so glad I didn't call them. They worry too much about me and Hannah, anyway.'

There were more pictures in the box. 'Who's that?' he said, pointing to a photo of a girl in front of a brick building. She wore jeans and a sweatshirt and held an armful of books. A little beanie was perched on her head.

'This?' She looked at the photo. 'You don't recognize me? That's me in college. Have I changed that much? It seems like a million years ago.'

In the picture, she was smiling, a big, carefree smile.

She showed him some more pictures. 'That's my room-mate. What a boozer she was. And that was my best friend . . . this was the drama club . . .'

'Who's that?' He pointed to a tall, handsome guy with a tennis racket under one arm and his other arm around Mary.

'Oh, him. No one.'

He tried to take a closer look, but she put the pictures away. 'I don't know why I save that junk. School! Imagine – my biggest worry then was passing my courses. It was such a free, privileged life. You've got it now, Jeff.'

'Me!' He didn't think of himself that way. Well . . . he was free. But privileged?

'You can do anything you want to with your life. Go anywhere. Try anything. You don't know how free you are.'

'Sometimes you can have too much freedom. I'd be glad if someone told me what to do.' But he knew he didn't mean it. 'In some ways, my parents had it easier at my age. My father went into the military when he got out of high school and then college. That's what everybody did. College or work. You didn't have to figure things out. You went one way or you went the other.'

'I still think it's better today,' she said. 'It's harder because you've got to think more, but it's better because you've got a choice. Even me. I made a choice. I didn't have to have Hannah.'

As she spoke, he kept looking at her. Her voice was low and intimate.

Hannah cried out, and Mary rocked the crib. Then, in a whisper, 'I think about my father's life a lot. He came out of Hitler's concentration camps, you know.'

Jeff crossed his legs, knocking against her leg. She moved slightly. 'I heard your father speak once. It was really interesting.'

'He rarely talks about it . . . He's a sick man, now. His

heart. That's why I can't live at home. Too upsetting for him. After they moved to Florida, I lived with my aunt in Rochester for a while.' She gave a short explosive laugh, then looked over at Hannah. 'But that was too upsetting for me.' She lowered her voice. 'My aunt Alice.' She shook her head. 'She wanted me to go back to school and she was going to take care of Hannah. Take over is what she meant. I don't want anyone else bringing up my baby. I notice that since I've had Hannah, the whole world thinks it has a licence to give me advice and comment on my life. Anyway . . . here I am.'

He nodded sympathetically. He was sympathetic, he was listening, but he was also thinking about the guy in the picture. Was that Hannah's father? Did she still love him? She must have loved him once.

'Are you sorry?' he said.

'About Hannah?'

'No, that sounds stupid. Cut. Leave that footage on the floor. Sorry I said it.'

'Not that stupid. I am sorry sometimes.' She looked over at Hannah. 'Not about her, but the life . . .' She sighed. 'I admired myself in the beginning. I thought I was a heroine. Joan of the Babies. I was going to do everything – go to school, become an actress, be the world's best mother.'

'From what I've seen, you are a good mother.'

She smiled slightly. 'I'm okay. I have my good days. I'm not as brave as I thought I was, or as smart. All I know is, every day I wake up and it's always the same now.' She fell silent, rubbing her lips. 'My mouth is still a little numb . . . Sometimes when I think of what I was going to do . . . Nobody wanted me to have Hannah. Not even me, at first. That's hard to say now. But she wasn't real to me. Then I decided, I'm going to have her and I'm going to keep her. I don't know why I decided that, except she was there, waiting.'

She looked down at Hannah, who was sleeping with her mouth ajar. 'I don't know why I'm talking so much.'

He straightened up. 'Do I look bored?' Already, in his mind, it was the two of them against the world. The world thought she'd made a mistake. The world thought she wasn't a good mother. But he knew differently. She was alone. She was small. When he thought about how much bigger he was than she, it gave him a very tender feeling. He would put a fence between the two of them and the world. He would be her defender. Thinking this, it seemed as if his own life took on meaning. It grew and expanded. There was a purpose to everything. Now he knew why he was here and not in California.

His thought came tumbling in on him, exciting him. And her nearness excited him, the flesh of her upper arm, the smell of her hair. And her closeness – so close – did he dare? They were just beginning, everything was so new, so tentative, so fragile – the wrong word, the wrong look could ruin everything.

Hannah woke up with a cry. Mary took the baby on the bed to change her, then reached across Jeff for the box of nappies. Her outstretched arm, her five fingers, the plump wrist – all seemed to hang there, to speak to him. Nibble me, they said. Crazy thought.

He knew what he wanted, but what about her? Everything she did meant something for him, had a hidden meaning. He leaned over her arm, the investigator, a reader of hidden signs and signals, a quivering detective of the heart, a Sherlock Holmes of passion.

'Diaper,' she said.

He handed it over.

'That little squirrel shirt.'

He gave her that.

She put the shirt on Hannah. 'You are a friend,' she said.

What could he do but agree?

13

He went over to the Belcos' often. Very often. She never called him. What was he supposed to do, wait till she had another toothache? She was so casual with him. When he was there, he was there. 'Oh, hi,' she'd say, like there you are and so what? Did she want him to make the first move? That had already gotten him into trouble. He was so full of heat and she was so cool . . .

Did she think he was deprived, that he hung around her because – *poor guy doesn't know any other girls*. Maybe he had to send her another message. Stay away for a while, then come walking up the street with a few women he knew. Jeff and a few of his close friends – Jill, Robin, Ginny, Rebecca . . . There were so many girls dying to go out with him, he scheduled them in small, manageable groups, A to D on Monday, E to H on Tuesday, and so on.

Fade in: Mary at the window, watching Jeff . . . *Close on* Mary's fingers clutching the curtain . . . Great scene, but the jealous one was him. Who was he jealous of? Danny, his best friend. How was that for craziness? But weren't they in that house together when he wasn't there? Every morning? Every night? All through the night?

One afternoon he arrived and found the two of them in the living room, she cozily perched on the arm of Danny's chair. For all he knew they'd been all over each other a second before he appeared. Mary was barefoot, wearing only shorts and a shirt, her hair loose like she'd just got out of the shower. She doesn't have a bra on, he thought. Bang! It felt like somebody had socked him in the stomach. 'Oh, hi,' she said, and turned back to Danny.

'Just write something, Danny,' she said. 'Get started on that comp.'

Danny looked down at the notebook at his feet. 'I can't write five hundred words about my goals. I can't get more than five words on that. Who's thinking about ten years?'

'You must have some long-range plans,' Mary said. 'Hannah doesn't, the cat doesn't, but you – you must have some plans.'

'The army. We might have a war. I might be dead.'

'Come on,' Mary said, leaning over him. 'Don't be so negative. Write something. You only have to start. Think about all the things you'd like to have. Dream a little.'

Dream! Jeff knew just what Danny was dreaming about the way he was hunched over Mary's bare legs. Jeff walked out to clear his head. When he came back, Mary was in the kitchen warming up Hannah's bottle. 'Oh, hi,' she said, again. 'Danny's in the living room.' Then she went upstairs.

Maybe she thought he came to see Danny, but everyone else knew why he was there. Mrs. Belco had been giving him the evil eye for days. One afternoon she stopped him on the way in and asked him to walk her to the car.

'I'm worried about you, Jeff. You know what I'm talking about?'

'College?'

'Don't be so dumb. That girl has problems. Big problems. Alone with a baby. There's a something missing in her life and it's wearing pants. And then you walk in. You're a good-hearted kid, but just remember you're not responsible for the world. Let her figure out her own life. Show her you're interested and she'll grab on to you like glue.'

He wouldn't have minded if Mary had stuck to him a little, but Mrs. Belco was wrong. Mary wasn't the clinging sort.

Friday night was Sadie's busiest time. Families came in for Sadie's famous fish dinners. The smell of deep fries filled the restaurant, and Jeff sent rack after rack of dishes through the machine. He didn't begin to catch up till after nine-thirty. At ten o'clock he started pulling the machine apart and cleaning the pipes. 'Hey, chef?' Danny said, looking in. 'I found a cockroach in my clam chowder.'

'No extra charge.'

'Come on out here. I want you to meet somebody.'

Jeff followed him into the restaurant. Tracy and another girl were sitting at one of the front booths.

'This is my cousin, Dawn,' Tracy said.

'Hi.' Dawn waved her hand. She had a long narrow face and was wearing the same bright red lipstick as Tracy and the same blue eyeshadow. Even their fingernails were alike.

Danny walked Jeff back to the kitchen. 'You like Dawn?' He slapped him on the ass. 'Get a move on. We're all going to the Red Barn.'

Jeff picked up a rack of cups and stacked them on the shelf.

'What are you doing?' Danny said.

'I'm working.'

'You're not chained to that machine.' Danny gave him a winning smile. 'What am I going to do with two of them? Anyway, I promised Tracy I'd get you. She wants her cousin to have a good time. Are you going to ask Sadie or do I do it?'

'She'll throw you out on your butt.' He was mopping when Danny came back.

'It's all set,' Danny said. 'Just clean up.'

'You're kidding.'

Danny smiled into his moustache. 'You have to know how to talk to older women. And that takes an experienced, mature man.'

'That describes you?' Jeff finished in a hurry. He wasn't one to turn down a good time.

The four of them crowded into the front of Danny's truck. That warmed things up right away.

'Tight squeeze,' Dawn said, breathing on him. She smelled minty.

'My big feet.'

She straightened herself out. 'My legs.'

Her legs were what he couldn't take his eyes off. They were resting against his. Everytime she moved, more of her came in contact with Jeff. They didn't have to meet. They'd met. He had the window open and his arm out, but he was burning. Full body contact. He wasn't complaining.

She sniffed. 'I smell fries.'

'That's me, it gets right in my hair.' He stuck his head out the window. 'I smell like the kitchen. I should .have gone home and showered.'

'No, I like it. It makes me hungry.' Her earrings brushed against his cheek. He stuck out his tongue and licked her ear. She shrieked.

'Is he being bad?' Tracy said. 'Jeff, I told her you'd be good.'

The parking lot at the Red Barn was packed. Dawn leaned on Jeff's arm. Was she one of those women who liked to hang onto a man? The comparison to Mary was unavoidable.

Inside they sat at the bar, waiting for a table. Vet, who lived upstairs at the Belcos', was at the bar dressed in running shorts and a sleeveless tight black shirt. He promised to come by and see them later.

It was midnight before they were seated. Jeff was hungry, and they ordered a double pizza with everything. Danny ordered a pitcher of beer. By the second pitcher, they all started getting happy. Tracy cuddled up with Danny, who kept winking at Jeff.

'Want to dance?' Jeff asked. On the floor, Dawn closed her eyes. They danced close. Their legs kept touching and she was hanging on him really hard. Even after the music stopped, they kept dancing. When they went back to the table, Tracy and Danny were gone. 'I like you, Jeff,' Dawn said. 'Tracy told me I would.' They sat there and kissed until Tracy and Danny came back.

'Oh, great,' Tracy said, smiling. 'Leave you two for a second. I told you he was a smoothie.'

Jeff slid his glass through the wet places. He should have felt happier than he did.

Vet stopped by their table, rubbing Danny's back. 'Introduce me to the ladies.' He sat down next to Dawn. 'Let me see your fingernails,' he said taking her hand. 'Wild. You two girls look like sisters. Don't they look like sisters, Danny? If there's anything prettier than one pretty lady, it's two pretty ladies.'

Dawn was like a cat lapping up Vet's compliments. Smiling and laughing at everything he said. Jeff felt like the fifth wheel and got up and took a walk. It wasn't a smart thing to do. Not if he wanted to hold onto Dawn. At every table, people were singing and yelling. He walked out into the parking lot to clear his head and his lungs and his ears – and his brain, too. He was thinking about Mary again, Mary alone in the house. Would she have come to the Red Barn if he'd asked her? The five of them? With Vet joining the party, it would have been six. Dawn and Vet. Him and Mary.

He caught a ride back to the city with a guy on his way home from work. 'I work nights, too,' Jeff said. The man dropped Jeff at the corner of Spring Street, a long walk home, but a short block to the Belcos'. It was really late, too late for anyone to be up. He was just going to pass the house and keep going.

There was a light on in the hall, but the rest of the house was dark. He heard something, the porch swing creaking. Mary was sitting there, slowly rocking Hannah in her lap. A dark Madonna, her hair down around her shoulders and flowing into the darkness. Her being here at this hour was magical, as if she'd known he'd be coming and was waiting for him.

He leaned on the step. 'Hello,' he said softly. 'What are you doing up so late?'

'The room is so hot.'

'It's cool here.'

'Perfect.'

He sat down. He was tired.

'Are you coming from work?'

'Well, sort of . . .' Yeah, he thought, you go out, you get smashed, you do stupid things, you start kissing Tracy's cousin.

They sat there for a long time. There were long silences. Once she reached down and touched his hair. 'Sleeping?' She talked on and off, and he listened, sitting on the steps with his head on his knees. She talked about her family a lot. Some of it was interesting. Mostly, though, it was boring, things he'd heard before.

He fell asleep a couple of times, just dropped off for a moment. He was thinking about that guy again, the one in the picture she'd shown him, the guy with the tennis racket. Good looking, with a high opinion of himself, used to getting everything he wanted. Smooth, easy, with a lot of glitter and a mile-long line of chatter, the kind of guy who could talk a girl into bed . . .

It was nearly morning before he left. It was cool, and the grass was wet. What he remembered before he dropped off to sleep was her stroking his head. It had been so natural, so kind, so easy. He had kept his eyes closed. It had only been a moment. He remembered it and then he slept.

14

'What are you doing?' Mary said over the phone. It was late one morning. He had been doing a bit of developing in the cellar when the phone rang. 'Are you coming over?'

'Do you want me to?'

'That's why I called you.'

'I'll be right there.'

All the way over, he tried to figure it out. No crisis, it wasn't raining, and she didn't have a toothache. All he could think was that he hadn't been to the Belcos' for a couple of days, but when had that bothered her before?

She and Hannah were waiting for him in front of the house. 'Are you up for a walk?' she said. 'That's really what I want to do.'

'It's fine with me. What's the problem?'

'No problem.'

'You mean you just called me? Maybe you don't know this, but this is an historic moment.'

'It is?'

'Mary called Jeff.'

'Didn't I ever call you before? Sure, I called you.'

'When you had a toothache. That doesn't count. How come you called today?'

'Would you believe — I missed you? It's dull around here without you. Have you been busy?'

'I've been working at Sadie's and I'm still painting the house. And last night I was up all night developing pictures of my parents' thirty-fifth anniversary.'

'Then you're tired . . .'

'Not anymore.'

They walked. They talked. He didn't notice where they went or what he said or even what she said. It didn't matter. She'd called him. She wanted him around.

72

After that he was over at the Belcos' every chance he had. No more Oh, hi's. She was waiting for *him* and off they'd go, walking, or to the park, or to the Mall. Sometimes he admitted to himself that she needed someone to talk to and there he was, convenient as a backscratcher. He still didn't know where he stood with her, but it was another place. Another country.

Before, they'd been like two uneasy countries, wary and stiff with each other, all boundaries and border crossings closely guarded. But now there was this miraculous thaw, the ice had melted, the borders were open. Diplomatic talks were going on about areas of mutual interest.

What did she have for breakfast, he wanted to know. 'I eat a substantial breakfast,' he said.

'Not me. I never eat breakfast, maybe some juice. Mostly nothing. I don't get hungry till lunchtime.'

'You can miss lunch, but breakfast is basic.'

She laughed at him. 'Yes, comrade.'

'Why comrade? Because I'm Russian?'

'No, because you've got a plan for everything.'

'Don't you?'

'I wish I did.'

'Morning is my best time for thinking,' he said.

'In the morning I don't think about anything.'

'That's because you don't eat a substantial breakfast.'

They argued a lot. He liked to get her going and she liked to disagree. 'Think of it, Mary, we have so much to say to each other.'

'Like what?'

His mind leaped to a long agenda of questions he had mulled over, but was she ready to talk about everything? Such as, did she like a hard bed or a soft bed? He leaned toward the hard, but knowing her she was probably just the opposite. What about nightclothes? He was ready to give up sleeping in his underwear. Didn't she think naked was best?

'Showering,' he said tactfully. 'How do you feel about sharing a bathroom?'

'With whom?'

'With your roommate.'

'Oh, Hannah's fine.'

That wasn't exactly what he meant.

'Sleeping,' he said. 'What about sleeping?'

'Sharing again?'

'Ummm . . .'

'Ummm, what?'

'Ummm means I'd like to.'

'Don't get any ideas.'

But that was the trouble – all he had was ideas.

Still, talk was progress. Talk filled in the spaces, the gaps, the silences, coloured in the outlines of the picture. They were finding out about each other.

Sometimes, though, there were things he wished she wouldn't tell him – even though he wanted to hear them. Like how hot it was in her attic room and how she'd stood in the shower so long, Mrs. Belco had yelled at her. 'It's the hottest part of the house, I wish she wouldn't forget that. But she complains because I'm running two fans. Well, poor Hannah! She's got a heat rash. I have to leave her on the sheet with nothing on.'

Nothing on . . . nothing on . . . nothing on. He got stuck there. It was like a radio jingle. Why was she telling him that stuff? Because she was relaxed with him. Because they were friends. Because she trusted him. But oh, his lascivious imagination!

He was crazy. He knew he was crazy. It was hormones, but knowing it didn't help.

Sometimes, walking around or crossing streets or in doorways, they bumped into each other. He loved bumping. One of life's unexamined pleasures. There were shoulder bumpers and hip bumpers and rear bumpers, too. Did he bump into her or did she bump into him? Did it matter?

74

What did she feel about bumping? It was a subject he never brought up with her, but he knew she liked it, too. She wasn't complaining, was she? Or disappearing, or trying to get away from him. Was she bumping back? Mutual bumping was the best kind of bumping.

'Hi, it's me again.'

'Hi! I've been waiting for you.' Mary was outside, holding Hannah in one arm and wrestling the stroller down the stairs.

'Let me,' he said manfully, grabbing the stroller and jumping the five porch steps. He came down on the side of his foot and turned his ankle. 'Ouch!'

'Serves you right – what'd you grab the stroller for?'

He hopped around. 'I wanted to help.'

'Orloff's friendly service. Next time, wait till I ask.'

'How about a little sympathy?'

She rubbed his shoulder, her hand lingering. 'Better?'

'Very good.' He had an instant, unauthorized, illegal reaction. 'More?'

'Enough.' She put Hannah in the stroller. 'I'm going to the market. Are you coming with me?'

'What's your guess?'

'You're coming.'

It was dry and hot, midday, their bodies cast no shadows. A passing bus raised a cloud of dust. 'Hannah's father,' he asked in a casual tone, 'what was he like?'

'What brought that subject up?'

'Nosy.' He pushed his nose self-consciously, his busted beak. 'You heard of Pike's Peak? This is Orloff's.'

'I like your nose better than mine.'

He dismissed his nose with a wave of his arm. Brushed across it so hard his eyes smarted.

'You hit yourself,' she said. 'And you're bleeding. I don't believe this. First your ankle, now your nose. Lie down before you bleed all over yourself.'

He looked around. 'Here? On the sidewalk?'

'You want to stop that nosebleed? Put your head way back,' she said professionally. 'I used to get nosebleeds all the time when I was little.' She knelt over him. 'Pinch it.'

'You know so much,' he said admiringly.

'You worry me. Are you always such a klutz?'

He looked up at her. Doctor Silver, slightly sweaty. Heartshaped angel face. It would have been so easy to embrace her, here on the sidewalk with people walking around them. 'Say it again, what did you call me?'

'Klutz. As in he who falls over his own feet.'

'That's what I thought you said.'

She touched his nose. Oh, that touch, those warm, careful fingers, those eyes, that little furrow of tender concern. 'Does it hurt?'

'A little. You'd make a wonderful doctor.' Mary peering up his nose. 'Isn't this romantic?'

He waited with Hannah in a patch of shade outside the market while Mary went in for some crackers and a candy bar. His ankle ached a little, but his nose felt all right. When Mary came out, he suggested they take the bus and ride over to Thornden Park. 'It's going to be a lot cooler over there.'

On the bus, the three of them shared the chocolate bar. Hannah took her whole piece in her mouth. 'No,' Mary said and tried to get it out of Hannah's mouth. Even though he'd sworn off sweets, Jeff couldn't resist the chocolate because Mary had given it to him.

'So what's his first name?' he said.

'Who?'

'You know.'

'I'm not going to tell you.'

'Why not? Is it a beautiful name like Orloff?'

'If I told you, you'd know his mother.'

'Is she famous?'

'I'm not telling you.'

'Is she an actress?'

'I'm not telling you.'

'What is there, only one actress in the world?'

'His name is Paul.'

He felt the chocolate's sweetness drip in the back of his throat. Too sweet. 'Is he smart? Good looking?' Innocent questions, but in his heart all he wanted to hear was bad news.

'Paul, good looking? He thought so. Hannah, sit still, you're kicking me. We're almost there.' Then, 'Paul loved taking care of himself, staying in shape.'

'In love with himself.'

'Not really. I wouldn't say that. Well – I suppose so – maybe a little, but who isn't?'

Jeff's heart sank. She was defending him, still interested. He heard it in the intensity that came into her voice. 'You two – it must have been heavy duty.'

'Heavy duty! I hate that expression.'

'I mean, were the two of you . . . was it . . .' Hannah stood and grabbed at his face.

Mary pulled her back. 'Stop it now.'

Why didn't he say what he meant? 'You and Paul – was it the real thing?'

'Let's drop it. It's not exactly my favourite subject.' But a moment later she came back to it. 'Paul was all right. He tried to help me.'

'Yes, I'm impressed. He let you have the baby alone.'

'What was he supposed to do? He couldn't have it for me.' The bus stopped and they watched a couple of women get on. 'He didn't want me to have the baby,' Mary said. 'So why would I want him around? He didn't want to be there, and I didn't want him there.'

'Didn't he want to marry you?'

'What do you mean?' The look she gave him – lightning bolts from under her brows. 'Jeff, where are you coming from? Marriage, who's talking about marriage? It's bad

enough the way things happened, but marriage! I didn't
want to marry him. I would never have married him.'

15

They hopped off the bus above the campus, near the entrance to Thornden Park. It was blazing in the sun. The tennis courts and swings were nearly empty; everyone was under the trees or by the pool. They settled down on the hillside overlooking the swimmers. Kids were jumping and diving into the water. There were other couples around with little kids. Did he and Mary and Hannah look like they belonged together? The Family – he framed them in the camera's eye. Mother, Father, Child. Mother and Father observing Child, who is now halfway down the hill. Mother pursues Child and brings her back under protest. Father distracts Child with finger play.

Had it just been Mary and him, they could have been anything – sister and brother, cousins, friends – but with Hannah they were The Family.

Where would they live? They'd have to move out of the Belcos'. Get an apartment of their own. They'd live here, near the campus, and on hot days like this they'd come to the park. They wouldn't have a lot of junk in the apartment. They'd each bring their own mattresses, and there'd be Hannah's stuff. And a big refrigerator divided down the middle because they liked to eat different things. They'd eat on the floor. No, that would gross Mary out. Wooden boxes for a table and chairs. Lots of boxes at Sadie's, and she'd never miss a couple of forks and spoons. He was sure she'd let him have all the cracked dishes they needed. She was always telling him to throw away any chipped mugs he found.

'What are you looking so pleased about?' Mary said, tickling his arm with a blade of grass.

'I was furnishing an apartment.'

She looked interested. 'You're moving out?'

'I might. Would you like to share a place?'

'Maybe I'll be looking sooner than you. That room is impossible. I don't think I can go through the whole summer up there. And Mrs. Belco—'

'What's the matter with her?'

Mary laughed and took a wad of dirt out of Hannah's mouth. 'Oh, her – she's all right, I guess. She means well. People who give advice always mean well, but it's not always easy to take.'

Later, Mary bought hot dogs, soda and popcorn at a stand and fed Hannah little pieces of hers.

'You feed her much of that stuff?' he said. 'Fried foods, processed meat, bologna – all that junk is full of chemicals.'

'You're eating it.'

'Just being sociable.'

Mary wiped mustard off Hannah's mouth. 'Do you have something to say about everything? I'll tell you right now, Jeff, I like cream-filled cakes, jellies with whipped toppings, and any kind of homemade pie, with maple walnut ice cream. Whenever I get the urge, I have something sweet.'

'I do too,' he admitted, 'but then I do penance. After today, it's going to be shredded wheat for breakfast all week.'

'I'd rather eat Brillo.'

On the way back to the bus, they went into Waverly Hall and wandered through the cool, nearly empty corridors. Looking past a folded-back wall, they discovered klieg lights overhead and an empty stage, chairs knocked this way and that as if the actors had just been there but had fled when they appeared. Mary hung back, but Jeff hopped up on the stage.

'On the stage, cast!' He clapped his hands. 'Mary, put that child down. It's improvisation time. I want you to make believe you're walking down the street and I'm following you.'

'Come on, Jeff, let's go.'

'We're improvising. You don't know me, and I'm making some moves toward you.'

'Jeff—'

'Mary, come on. I remember you used to love improv time in high school.'

'That was then. This is now. I'm through with all that.'

'Come on, Mary, just play along.'

'Jeff, maybe if you could act. Is that supposed to be a lecherous look?'

'Pretend you don't know the way.'

'Do you know the way?'

'Do I know the way!'

'That's what I just said.'

'I know the way. What way do you want to know, baby?'

'Do I know the way, baby!' Mary held her sides laughing, and then Hannah started laughing and shrieking.

'Cut! I'm the director, but if you're going to laugh at everything I say, farewell!' He stepped off the stage and came down on his sore ankle.

'Awww!' Mary said sympathetically.

He held himself upright on the back of a chair. 'Pain, pain . . . Mary, have you really given up acting?'

She sat down next to him. 'Seriously? I can't think about it now. I have to think about Hannah. I have to be realistic.'

'Realistic.' He spat out the word. That was parent talk. Be realistic, be sensible, down to earth, find a solid, well-paid profession. Realistic! A conniving word. 'What's wrong with flying? What's wrong with dreaming a little? What's wrong with Mary Silver, leading lady?'

'It sounds like a soap opera to me.' Mary stood up, straightened her jeans, and paced across the stage. Suddenly she was the leading lady. With a large, grand motion she swept up an imaginary gown.

Then in an instant she switched, going slack and loose,

squatting down, knees wide. 'Hey, man. Hey, man, give me a drink.'

It was good. Jeff applauded.

Mary threw him a kiss. The leading lady was back. Then she sat down again with Hannah between her legs.

'That was great,' he said.

'No.' She shook her head. 'That's just amateur stuff. There are so many talented people around, and they're all working hard, getting better. What's my so-called talent worth? You can have all the talent in the world, but if you're not out there doing it . . . By the time I get back to acting, I'm going to be so far behind I'll never catch up.'

It drove him crazy listening to her. 'If you want to be an actress, you will be an actress. Helen Hayes was five feet tall, too short they told her, but that didn't stop her. She said she made up her mind she was going to act, no matter what. She acted tall and she got the part of Mary Stuart, the tallest queen in history. Six feet tall.'

'I'm not Helen Hayes.'

'No, you're Mary Silver, and you – you, Mary Silver – can be anything you want. I'm talking about the future. I'm talking about aspirations. I'm talking about thinking big.'

'Think big for yourself. I don't understand you. What difference does it make to you what I do?'

He didn't even know himself. All he knew was he had doubts about himself, but none about Mary. He talked big, but what was he but a dreamer who veered between belief in his talent and disbelief. He was on a seesaw. It was only with Mary that he had a long, steady view. She was talented. She could succeed. Somehow, believing in her made it possible for him to believe in himself.

On the way out of the building, Mary stopped to read the bulletin board. 'Here, Jeff, did you see this?' She pointed to a notice. 'This is for you. Look who's coming here. Francis McLaren – isn't he one of your famous directors?'

'Francis McLaren?' Jeff read the notice. The Friends of the Cinema were doing a Francis McLaren retrospective at the Everson Museum, and McLaren himself was going to be there to answer questions. 'This is fantastic. He must by eighty-five by now. Still making movies, too.'

His eye caught another notice. SARANAC LAKE ACTING WORKSHOP. 'Hey, Mary! Wait, here's something for you. Listen to this. "Four-day acting workshop," ' he read. ' "Work intensively with Broadway professionals." What do you say, Mary? You go up there, those professionals see you, you're going to be discovered.'

'Come on, Jeff. Don't start again.'

'It's fate,' he insisted. 'You saw something for me, then I saw something for you. You're getting a message from the stars, excuse the pun.'

Hannah started beating her heels against the stroller rail. 'The only message I'm getting,' Mary said, 'is that Hannah's tired. We better go.'

'Wait a minute, Mary, I mean it. This is perfect. We were just talking about opportunity, and here it is. You feel out of it? Everyone's getting ahead of you? Well, here's your chance to catch up.'

'You don't make up a year in four days.'

'Four days could change your life. When they see what talent you have and you get a little encouragement—'

'What am I going to do with encouragement? Play Lady Macbeth for Hannah?'

'Oh, are you negative.'

'Realistic.'

'That word again. It makes me crawl.'

'Jeff, come on. I can't do this.'

'You can.'

'Think about me, Jeff. This is Mary. Mother Mary. They don't want actors with babies.'

'You don't know that.'

'Oh, Jeff, what am I going to do with you?'

He studied the notice. 'You've still got ten days to apply.'

'Ten days or ten years, I still can't do it.'

'Do you want to do it, or don't you? That's the question.'

'Do I want to do it?' She pushed her hands through her hair. 'The truth? I'd love to do it. To act, to feel that I was learning. To be in that world again.'

'So you admit it!'

She leaned against the wall and took a deep agonized breath. 'Why are you doing this to me, Jeff? Do you know how hard this is for me? I've had to give up things . . . Sure, I want it. That's the trouble, I've never stopped wanting. But I told you, I can't think about it.'

'I'd drive you there. Saranac Lake isn't that far.'

'Drive me? You don't have a car.'

She was being realistic again. 'There are no problems, Mary. The only problem is in your head. Say yes and I'll have a car.' He was intoxicated by the power of his own words. 'If I have to, I'll buy a car.'

'Sir Walter Jeff. Your magic cape is showing.' She pushed the doors open. 'Let's go, Walter.'

He tore the notice down and caught her between the double doors. 'You want me to call these people for you?'

Her lips tightened. She looked angry, and then she started to smile, her eyes darting across his face. 'You never give up, do you?' Eyes full of doubt and excitement. She took the notice. 'If I do anything, I'll do it myself.'

She leaned against the outside door. They were pressed together between the doors, on their way out, between the inner door and the outer door, not in, not out. More than friends, but not that much more. Close, but not that close. He leaned toward her. Her lips were where his lips were. He was aware of her breath and the faint smell of mustard and of Hannah burbling and dust in the air and his elbow jammed against the door.

'Good grief,' she said, pushing the door open, 'that was nice.'

16

'Mary?' Jeff stood at the top of the attic stairs and announced himself. 'Hey, Mary, it's me.' It was after supper. Her door was open.

'Wait a minute.'

He heard her moving around inside. A moment later, she came to the door. She was barefoot, wearing a white shift. 'Come on in.'

He took a step into her room and the baby smells hit him. Ammonia, baby powder, baby puke. Was romance really possible?

Her room was stifling. On the floor, two fans whirred. He was too big for the room, out of proportion. 'This room is like a sardine can.'

Mary set Hannah on the floor. 'I told you. The heat collects all day.' She towelled the film of sweat from her forehead. The baby was wearing just a little nappy. Mary stood her up. 'Watch this.' Hannah shuffled her feet excitedly, and with Mary holding her hands, she wobbled toward Jeff. 'Isn't that exciting? She's beginning to walk.'

He knelt down. 'See if she'll come to me. Come on, Hannah,' he urged. 'Let go of her hands, Mary.' Hannah started toward him, took a step, then went down. Mary picked her up and kissed her.

He walked around the room, holding his breath. He wanted Mary, but Hannah came with the package. Why couldn't he just have Mary? He loved her. Was it love? Oh, this was deadly. He couldn't think. He wanted Mary. He wanted her! He wanted, he wanted, he wanted.

'Want to do something?' he said.

They went down to the lake and followed the curving path near the plum trees. The sun had set, but it was still light. Hannah slept in the stroller.

'Did you call them?' he asked.

'I'm not thinking about it,' she said.

'Then how come you know what I'm talking about?'

'Pretty hard not to! That's all you talked about the other day.'

'Okay, today we talk about other things. We'll talk about—'

'What?'

Us, he thought. There was a breeze from the lake, and he kept noticing dim, secluded spots where they could stop and relax and maybe take their clothes off.

'Do you want to sit down? That looks like a good place,' the hypocrite said, pointing to where bushes would hide them from the path.

They found a grassy spot, and Mary set the brake on the stroller and sat back, leaning on her elbows. 'It's quiet here, cool . . . I can breathe . . . I'm so glad to be out of there.' She kicked off her sandals. 'Well, what are we talking about, Professor?'

'Nature. Man and nature. Man, woman and nature.' The hypocrite pointed to the lake, to the clouds, to the chimneys on the other side outlined against the yellow sky. The every-friendly parkway guide. Pointing out the important landmarks: the makeshift walls of the French Fort, the pond and the little bridge over it. 'That's where we used to fish . . . and there's where we picked wild plums and apples.' He pointed, he moved his arm, he knelt down next to her. The Guide. The Professor of Fruit and Passion. She'd pulled the shift up over her knees. He drew a leaf of grass lightly over her bare leg. He leaned toward her. Kiss? Was she in the mood? He had the need to touch her, to lie down next to her and put his arms around her and press himself against her.

He admired the rings she was wearing, raising her hands so the stones caught the light. She let him hold her hand, but when he let go, she let go. It was depressing. Where was the counterpressure? The enthusiasm? He hadn't stopped thinking about that kiss. *Good grief! That was nice.* Well, it could be a whole lot nicer.

I'm on my knees next to you. In a prayerful position. I bow down to you. I am wild for you. My heart and my prick, I offer them both to you. I worship your knees. I want you to raise your shift, pull it over your head. Are you wearing anything underneath? We're alone (except for the baby). I kick off my sneakers for you. My feet are bare for you. Look how I wiggle my toes invitingly. Don't you think I'm sexy? If you take off your clothes, I'll take off mine.

She was looking up at the sky, lying with her arms back, the flat circles of her breasts tight against the cloth. The breeze and the lights of cars moved through the bushes.

Why was she waiting for him to make the first move? Where was the liberated woman? He was trembling, filled with desire and doubt. He wanted her. How had he waited this long? He'd been fantastically patient. Enough!

She turned toward him with a pleasant expression. 'It's really nice here.'

He moved closer.

'Don't you love that sky, Jeff? Look, there's the first star.'

He was looking at her arm, the curved line of her throat, the awkward thrust of her shoulders. 'I love you,' he said.

She skipped a beat. 'Come on, Jeff, what do you know about love?'

'As much as you do. I say I love you – or whatever you call it.'

She smiled. 'I've got another name for it.'

He bent forward, committed, and put his hands over her breasts.

Her head came up and banged him in the nose. What a hard, bony head she had. His poor nose! The blow took the passion right out of him. It made him furious. He wanted to rap her back. And then his nose started to bleed.

She was up on her knees now. 'Your stupid nose is bleeding again!'

'Do you want me to lie down?' He lay down.

'I don't know what I want. I think I'm mad. I am mad. I'm confused. Your nose is bleeding. What am I supposed to do? The only thing I know is I don't want you crawling all over me.'

'What's the matter with me?' he said.

'You! You're not six years old. Who invited you to put your hands on me?'

He sat up and tasted blood in his throat.

She pushed him down. 'Stay right there. Don't talk.' She handed him a nappy. 'Stuff that up your nose.'

She was definitely annoyed.

'You had to try, didn't you? Big macho male. You feel better now?'

He'd suffered a setback. He regrouped and tried another tack. 'It's not just me who wants this, is it?'

'What do you mean? Who else is there? Have I been sending you that kind of signal? Did I indicate ever that I wanted . . . I hate this, it sounds like I'm anti-sex, and I'm not.'

'Just anti me.'

'No, that's not true, Jeff. I'm not starting anything with you, or anybody else, either. I just can't deal with that in my life right now.'

They started back, she silent and pushing the stroller along rapidly. He strode along beside her, quiet but cheerful. No hard feelings. No pouting. No resentment. He knew where she was coming from. She needed more time. He could live with that. 'So we're still friends,' he said. 'Friends, like in friends, friends, friends.'

'I don't know.'

He felt under his nose for blood. 'I understand,' he said. 'You hate me temporarily.'

'Oh, Jeff! Why can't you stay on the level. Your friendship means a lot to me. I don't want to lose that. But it's got to be like you said. Friends, like in friends, friends, friends.'

'Right.'

'Can you handle it?'

'I can,' he said. 'No problem. None.'

When they got back to the house, candles were flickering in the windows. The power had blown, and all the lights were out. Everybody was downstairs, but as soon as they saw Mary, they came rushing out.

'We had to disconnect two fans in your room,' Mrs. Belco cried, 'and your stereo was on.'

'What's the fuss?' Mary said. 'What'd you do, blow a fuse?'

'It could have been a fire. You've got too many appliances. I keep telling you. Those fans and that hair dryer. They're all out of your room, now.'

'You went into my room?' Mary ran upstairs.

Mrs. Century stood in her doorway like a ghost. 'Is everything all right? I just put on my television and everything turned off.'

'Ever since that one moved in,' Vet said, 'we've been overloaded.'

'Don't worry, I'm going to straighten her out. She's not going to burn my house down.' Mrs. Belco, shielding a candle in her hand, led the way upstairs. 'Mary?' she called. 'Mary. I want to talk to you.'

They all crowded into the attic stairs. Jeff tried to get ahead of them. He had a strange feeling that he had lived this moment before. The narrow stairs, the poor light, the screaming in the house . . . and upstairs she was waiting . . . It was a scene from a movie about the French Revolution. The mob had cornered the king and queen,

Marie Antoinette and Louis XVI, and was racing up the stairs to get them.

He heard Mary's door open, and then on the landing above him he saw her bare feet. That sight – those long, narrow, vulnerable, defenceless feet – devastated him. Ever since the park, he'd been saying to himself, Friends, friends, friends. And now everything came flooding back, everything he'd felt from the beginning. Mary . . . Mary . . . Mary . . . Mary.

17

Jeff lay on his back in the dark and wondered what was going to be between Mary and him. Whatever had gone wrong in the park (had anything gone wrong?), it wasn't his fault. He was just a normal, lusty, sexy, horny American male. What was she, un-American? Maybe he'd ask her, but not likely. Friends. He had to keep reminding himself. Friends . . .

When he went to see her, he ran, singing, I'm running to her, to my one true love . . . His heart sang. The running made him desire her more, and his prick sang. It was a duet. But when he was in sight of the house, he always slowed down and reminded himself – friends.

'I'm going to look for another place to live,' Mary said one day. 'I've had it here. Will you help me look?'

'No.'

Her face went wide with surprise. 'You won't?'

'I'm teasing,' he said hastily.

She handed him the newspaper with all the possibilities circled. 'Don't say anything about this to anyone yet. When I get a place, I'll tell them. What my parents pay Mrs. Belco, they can pay someone else.'

The first place they went to was advertised as a spacious one-room apartment on ground level. The room turned out to be in a cellar with two small windows looking out at a bare, stony yard. Everything smelled damp and mildewed. 'Cross that one off,' Mary said.

The second place advertised the view. They never got to see it. The man took one look at Hannah and shook his head.

After that, there was something wrong with every place. Most were too sleazy or babies made the landlords uneasy or they were too expensive. Jeff stood in the background, frowning a lot, trying to look authoritative, but then, afraid he'd was hurting Mary's chances, he smiled a lot, too.

It was getting really hot when they got to the last place, and they were both dragging. Hannah was fretful. 'Last is best,' Mary said. And it almost was. The house was on a quiet street with lots of trees and shade. A woman wearing shorts and a white T-shirt came to the door. When she saw Hannah, she beamed. 'Poor thing. It's so hot for her,' and she ran back to get them some water.

'I know how hard it is for young people today,' she said when she returned. 'Both my son and daughter are married, and they looked all over before they found anything. I only rent to couples with children. I feel—'

'No,' Mary interrupted. 'It's just me and Hannah. This is my friend.'

'Where's your husband?'

'It's just me and Hannah.'

Suddenly the woman remembered that she had promised to hold the apartment for someone else.

'Blessed are the hypocrites, for they shall prosper,' Jeff said, as they walked away.

They stopped at the House of Pancakes to use the bathrooms. Afterward they went to his house. It was cool in the back under the trees. Mary took off Hannah's clothes and let her go on the grass. She sat bent forward, holding her hair over her head. He ran his finger down her backbone.

She raised her head and shook it wearily.

'Okay,' he said.

She stretched out on the grass. He sat nearby. She was asleep when his mother came home. 'Who's this?' his mother said, leaning down to Hannah. 'Yes . . . what a little beauty.'

Mary sat up, tucking in her shirt. 'It was so hot I fell

asleep.' She picked up the baby. Her buttocks puckered against Mary's arm.

'Mum,' Jeff said, 'this is Mary Silver.'

Mary smiled. Jeff's mother kept looking from Mary to him. He could see the wheels turning. Mary is your friend? A friend with a baby. You never mentioned her, Jeff.

Sorry, Mum, I didn't want to give you a heart attack. No, *cut!* . . . Sorry, Mum, I was going to introduce you . . . *Cut!* We only met today . . . *Cut!*

And Hannah's father? Is he a friend of yours, too?

No, I never met him.

Just Mary?

Right, Mum. You got it.

'Can I hold her?' his mother asked Mary, who had dressed Hannah again. Hannah reached up her arms to be taken. 'Oh, she's so loving.'

'She's showing off for you, Mum.'

'Showing off! What an idea!' His mother hugged Hannah and kissed her neck. 'This little girl is full of love.' She sat down on the grass with Hannah and showed her the buttons on her dress, then made a little finger game for her.

'She likes you,' Mary said. 'She doesn't go to everybody that way.'

'I'm flattered.'

He didn't know quite how it happened, but his mother and Mary hit it off. They almost looked like sisters, both of them sitting there on the grass cross-legged and talking like old friends. 'I couldn't turn my back on Natalie when she was a baby,' his mother said. 'She'd wander off with anyone. Now, Jeff was the exact opposite. He wouldn't let me out of his sight.'

'I bet he was a cute little baby,' Mary said.

They both looked at him.

'Well . . . yeah,' his mother said. 'Cuter than he is now.'

When it was time for Mary to go, his mother said, 'Come and visit again. Anytime. Do you live far?'

'On Spring Street. I live with the Belcos.'

'Oh, the Belcos. Is that how you two know each other? Are you a relative?'

'No, I just live there.'

Before they left, his mother ran inside. She had a present for Hannah. 'This has been in my drawer forever,' she said, producing a narrow white box. Inside was a ceramic mobile with chickens, cows and roosters.

'I like Mary,' his mother said later. 'And that baby! It just makes me look forward to Natalie's having a baby.'

'They're not married yet, Mum.'

'As soon as they do, Natalie said they're going to work at it.'

'It sounds like a nine-to-five job.'

'When a woman gets to be thirty years old, she doesn't have time to waste. You know Natalie, she does things her own way. First a career, now marriage and a family. She plans, she thinks ahead. You could learn something from your sister.'

'You want me to have a baby, Mum?'

'I'll just ignore that,' his mother said.

The next day, he went to see the Francis McLaren movies at the museum. They were good, more than good, there was a clean, spare feeling to them. Jeff had a list of questions he meant to ask during the lecture, but first there was a short break. He went down to the basement, down a long flight of stairs to the men's room, and there was McLaren, the old man himself, hawking and clearing his nose. Here he was, alone with the Great Director, but Jeff was so awe-struck that he didn't say a word.

'Not a word?' Mary said to him afterwards.

'Not one word. What do you say to a great man when he's blowing his nose?'

18

'How would you like to go out with me Saturday night?' Jeff asked Mary. 'Billy Scroggs is at the Red Barn.'

'You mean a date? Do we have to have a date?' she said. 'Can't we just go?'

'No problem.' He walked away. Friends. 'No dates,' he said, coming back. 'No plans. If I come by Saturday, we'll just do something.'

'Fine with me.'

Saturday night he was there, dressed but not overdressed. A clean pair of jeans, a shirt with a little Western styling around the pockets and collar, a gold chain around his neck.

She was dressed just as casually, wearing a man's white shirt and a red tie around her waist, her hair loose. He had his mother's car – and Mary had Hannah. Surprise! He'd forgotten Hannah. She was dressed up, too. Blue overalls and clean white socks decorated with tiny bluebirds.

'You sure you want to take her? It's a beer joint.'

'I don't go anywhere without her.'

He went around behind the car and jumped on the fender. 'Can't you get a babysitter?' Big no date with Hannah chaperoning.

'When? Right now? I don't know anyone. Look, if you can't handle it—'

'Maybe my mother would take care of her.'

She just gave him a look.

'Bars and kids – you don't go to bars with kids.'

'What do you care how it looks, Jeff? I didn't think you were that conventional.'

Ouch. That hurt. He got behind the wheel. 'Everyone in. We take Miss Hannah along. You don't care, she don't care, I don't care. If anyone says anything about what she's got in the bottle, we show them her ID card.'

Mary was quiet on the drive over. In the parking lot at the Red Barn, she handed Jeff a letter. 'Read this.'

He turned on the dome light in the car and saw the letterhead. SARNAC LAKE THEATRE WORKSHOP. 'You wrote them!'

'I called them,' she said, 'and they wrote right back. They want me to come, they even offered me a partial scholarship.'

He started reading the letter. 'This is terrific.'

'Save the cheers. You see what they say at the end. They want me, but without Hannah. What does it say? There are no facilities, no arrangements, no place for a baby, and absolutely no time for anything but the workshop.'

He read the letter again. ' "We regret . . . If you can make alternate arrangements . . . " ' He handed the letter back to her. 'What's the problem, Mary? Hire somebody to take care of Hannah.'

'Who? And who pays?'

'Your family?'

'They're paying for everything already. They've gone the limit to help me.'

'I thought doctors were rich.'

'Think again. If you're sick, it doesn't matter what you are.'

'Damn!' he said.

'Oh, it's not that terrible. What's changed? Nothing. Let's go in.' She reached in back for Hannah. 'Come on, my little ball and chain.'

In the Red Barn, there was an incredible hubbub. The band was warming up the crowd. People were singing and banging their beer mugs on the table. Billy Scroggs wouldn't be on for a while. They found a table on the side against the wall, where they could watch everything and still have a place for Hannah. Mary set the car bed on a couple of chairs, then gave Hannah a bottle. The baby's eyes were everywhere.

They'd hardly got settled when Danny and Tracy appeared. 'Hey!' Danny hit Jeff on the head. 'Why didn't you tell me you were coming here?'

Jeff slapped back. 'Want to get your head handed to you?' He was a little down. Was it the letter? He'd started all this. Mary seemed to be a little moody, too.

'Sit down, Tracy,' Danny said. 'I'll get our drinks.'

'I don't need your permission,' Tracy said, sitting down next to Mary. She wore dangly pink plastic earrings, pink lipstick, and a fluffy pink angora sweater. 'I'm Tracy,' she said. 'That oaf I go around with didn't know enough to introduce us.'

'I'm Mary Silver. And this is Hannah Silver.'

'Hi, Hannah! Want to shake? No? Is it hard taking care of a baby, Mary? I'd be scared of the responsibility. What if you do something wrong?'

Mary smiled a little. Jeff tipped his chair back, his arms folded, watching Mary. 'When you have a baby,' Mary said, 'you're half frightened all the time. I thought it would go away, but it never does. But you do get better at things.'

'You don't look scared to me.' Tracy bent close to Hannah. 'Her eyes are so pure and perfect. They never need fixing, do they? No false eyelashes, no underliner, no brighteners. They're perfection itself.'

'What's wrong with your eyes?' Danny said, coming back with their drinks. 'You've got great eyes.'

Tracy took her drink and turned back to Danny.

'The hard thing about having a baby is—' Mary laughed—'they're always there.'

'That's what I've been trying to tell him. I don't see how you do it, Mary.'

'Everybody isn't as antsy as you,' Danny said.

Jeff glanced at Mary. They hadn't come here to watch Danny and Tracy slug it out. 'Want to dance?'

'Go ahead,' Tracy said. 'I'll watch the baby.'

On the dance floor, Mary put her hand lightly on his arm. 'Are they always that way?'

'I don't know what's going on. He's usually a pussycat with her.' He put his arm around Mary's waist, and they moved slowly among the dancers. His arm tightened around her as they responded to the music.

'This is the first time I've been dancing in ages,' Mary said. 'I'm glad we came.'

He got really happy, and then he heard himself say, 'I could take care of Hannah—'

'I'm not going, Jeff. I'm not even thinking about it.'

They walked back to the table arm in arm. Tracy was alone. 'Where's the man?' Jeff said.

'Roaming.' Tracy fiddled with her earring. Her eyes looked glittery, as if she had been crying. 'I'll be right back,' she said, and left.

Later, in the men's room, Jeff and Danny stood in front of the mirror. Danny kept glancing at Jeff, sighing, then smoothing his jaw. 'How are you and Mary making out?'

'Not the way you think.'

'Hey, Mother Jeff, I see you holding her baby.'

'You don't see anything. What's the matter with you tonight? You and Tracy—'

'Did she say anything to you?'

'About what? You'd have to be blind not to notice the way you two are biting each other.'

'Me and Tracy?' Danny smiled, a trembly sort of smile. 'You noticed? I thought we were hiding it pretty good.' He hesitated and looked around. 'We finally got caught. You follow me? And now she wants to get rid of it.'

'Tracy's pregnant?'

'She thinks so. She's doing the test, but it's pretty sure.'

'What are you going to do?'

'Don't go broadcasting it all over. I don't want my

mother to get wind of this. I know what I want to do, but Tracy—' He shook his head. 'She's something else.'

'She's the one who gets the baby.'

'I'm willing to do my part. It's my kid, too. I said I'd marry her.'

'She still gets the baby.'

Later, in the car, he slid over next to Mary so his face was close to hers. They kissed. It was one of those mutual kisses. Fifty-fifty. They each came halfway. They met at the fifty-yard line – and stayed there.

'We've got to cut this out, Jeff.' She moved away.

'Do we?'

'I do.'

'I don't?'

She laughed and yawned. 'I'm so tired.'

She and Hannah both slept.

He thought about Danny and Tracy. Whatever they decided to do, there was going to be something wrong. When two people didn't want the same thing, there was bound to be trouble. Then he thought about Mary. She was lying with her cheek against the back of the seat, trusting him to get her and Hannah home safely. It made him feel really good, peaceful and smooth, the way he sometimes felt early in the morning before the light.

When he pulled up at the house, Mary woke up.

'I'll help you with Hannah,' he said.

'No, that's okay, Jeff.' She gave him a kiss on the cheek. 'I had fun.'

He watched her go up on the porch, then bend, fumbling for the key. She looked small and alone standing on that dark porch. And then he remembered the top of the stairs . . . her bare feet . . . those vulnerable feet . . .

'Mary.' He got out of the car.

She turned. 'What is it?'

He stood on the bottom step, looking up at her. 'You go to the workshop. I'll take care of Hannah.'

She shook her head. 'Don't worry about it, Jeff.'

He picked up the car bed and followed her inside. 'I mean it. I want you to do it.'

'Sir Walter Teddybear.' She kissed him again. 'I just have to forget it, Jeff. Thanks for offering.' She took the car bed from him and went up the stairs.

19

Mrs. Belco backed her cab out of the driveway. 'How are you, Mrs B.?' Jeff called. He looked up to Mary's window.

'She's not there. Some guy came for her in an Audi Five Thousand. Really posh car. She went off with him.'

'Hannah, too? When are they coming back?'

'Ask her. She doesn't tell me anything.'

He went around to the barn where Danny split wood. The axe buried in a stump had begun to rust. Not much call for firewood in the middle of the summer. Jeff balanced a round of wood on end, then raised the axe. It had to be Paul, Hannah's father. Was this the first time he'd come to visit? It was the first time Jeff knew about it. He brought the axe down, then tossed the splits aside and grabbed another round.

He split wood at a furious rate. The sweat poured off his face and down his sides. He pulled his shirt off and tied it around his forehead. He was still splitting wood when Mary returned.

'Jeff!' Mary waved to him and he strolled over, wiping his face on his shirt.

'Paul came up to see Hannah,' Mary said. Didn't she stand straighter with Hannah on one arm, eyes bright, her hair whipping across her face? 'You look like you got a sunburn. What were you doing?'

'Splitting wood.'

'In the middle of the summer?'

'Winter's on its way,' he said lightly.

'I see.' She caught it. She saw immediately how reserved and cool he was, holding back, hurt but not weeping, not screaming. No recriminations, no tantrums. No beating the ground with his fists.

'I figured you'd be over today,' she said. 'but they came unexpectedly. I didn't have a chance to call.'

'Right.' He had a cool reply ready – a summer menu, cucumber and radish salad and gelatinous smiles. 'Communication failure. All the phones broke down at the same time.'

'What are you getting so sarcastic about?' Mary put Hannah down on the grass and sat back on the porch steps.

This was his cue to get off stage. Walk off, split, fade out. *Cut! Cut! Cut!* He was hurt, injured, bleeding. Show some pride and dignity, Orloff. Go! He looked off (*long shot*), then he looked at her (*zoom in*).

'Nice day for a drive.' (*Generous smile.*)

'Terrific.'

'Did Hannah enjoy it?'

'Very much.'

'Did he buy her ice cream?' (*Subtle comparison.*)

'Too early.'

'Too bad.'

They looked at each other. 'I don't know what we're fighting about,' she said finally.

'Are we fighting?'

Mary scooped up some gravel, then let it spill out between her fingers. 'If we're not, I'll tell you what happened. Do you want to hear about it?'

Did he? Maybe yes, maybe no. 'Of course I want to hear.'

'You sure?'

'Mmmm.' (*Dr. Orloff tunes in.*)

'That was an awful couple of hours,' she said.

'Was it?' (*Concerned frown.*)

'Paul came to see Hannah, and I got scared. I always worry he'll try to take Hannah away from me.'

'He can't do that.'

'There's still prejudice against unmarried mothers. I

don't know what that man is capable of. And he's got money.'

'So what did he want?'

'Just to see Hannah, thank God.' She held out her hand. 'Look at me shaking. If I could I'd never see him again.' She leaned back, clasped her hands and took a deep breath. 'I'm okay. I am okay, but right now I'm getting really sick thinking of how cheap Paul got off. No cramps for Paul, no morning sickness, no being sick to his stomach over the future. He made a baby. Tra la. He did his part, he shows up once a year and that's that.

'When I think of how much I liked him and how little I knew what kind of person he was . . . I thought I had judgment, I thought I knew something about characters.'

Jeff listened to her, sorry for her one second, then sorry for himself the next, because with all her anger, it was still Paul. Paul. He jumped up, then sat down again.

'What are you doing?' Mary said. 'Working out?'

'I'm jealous.'

'Of Paul?' She burst out laughing. 'You are a jerk. Didn't you hear anything I said? I can't stand the man. Man! What kind of man is he? He's no man. You're twice the man he is.'

He sat down on the steps, at her feet. Twice the man Paul was. An honest, unexaggerated assessment.

'Do you think he'd ever offer to take care of Hannah while I went to school?'

Jeff smiled modestly.

'I've been thinking about that, Jeff. That was really generous of you.'

'I meant it.' If he had money, he'd give it all to her, he wouldn't want anything in return. Well . . . maybe just a little appreciation.

'I know you did. That was what made it so wonderful.'

'The thirty-day free trial period is still available.'

She laughed. 'What do you know about babies?'

'Come on, I've watched you enough. What's the big deal? Besides, if you bring Hannah to my house, my mum will be there most of the time.'

'Supposing I do it – I'm just talking – what would you want in return?'

'*Moi?* Nothing.'

'Come on, Jeff, tell the truth.'

'Maybe your eternal, endless, everlasting love and gratitude.'

'That's what I call an even exchange.' She tapped him on the head. 'Sir Walter Teddybear. Supposing – now just supposing – we did it. You can't even change a diaper.'

'A challenge!' He brushed off his hands. 'Orloffs welcome challenges. Does she need to be changed?'

'She always needs to be changed.'

He carried out the operation on his hands and knees with Hannah on the grass. At first he was a little tentative. Hannah kicked, wrinkled up her face, and complained. How come he's changing me?

'Okay, hold still, Hannah. This is going to be a new Olympic record.' He slid off the wet diaper and snugged up a dry one.

'You changed a diaper,' Mary said. 'Congratulations!' She picked up Hannah again. 'Oh, Jeff, if you only knew how much I'd like to go to that workshop.' She looked down at Hannah. 'What good am I to her if I'm dissatisfied? You know, don't you sugar? I get moody and depressed and you know it. You know when I'm feeling good and when I'm feeling bad.' She turned to Jeff. 'I'm going to ask Hannah. I'm going to let her decide. Jeff, this is your last chance to back out.'

'Not me,' he said.

'Okay.' She stood Hannah up and held her around the middle. 'Hannah, look at Mummy. You're going to decide. Do you want me to go to the workshop? Do you want to stay with Jeff? Say if you don't want me to do it, Hannah.'

Hannah looked at Mary as if she understood every word. He couldn't believe it. Was Mary serious? Asking a baby! How could Hannah decide? And then, she reached up and grabbed her mother's cheek and pushed it up into a smile.

Mary bent down and kissed the baby, then looked at Jeff. 'You saw that. Hannah wants me to be happy. You're stuck, Jeff. I'm going to do it.' She stepped on his foot. 'Yeah, my prince in blue jeans, stuck!'

20

Jeff had promised Mary he'd ask his mother about Hannah's staying with them and then he forgot about it. Why? Well, why anything? He forgot, that was all. That's the way he was. He wasn't methodical, he wasn't organized. Methodical was his brother. Organized was his sister. Methodical and organized was his father. *He* did what he had to do when he had to do it. When Mary reminded him that she was leaving for the workshop in a couple of days, he 'remembered.'

'Is it still okay with your mother?' she said. 'I'm getting Hannah's things together.'

'No problem,' he said, unwilling to admit he hadn't asked yet. Not that he expected any problems. His mother was a good guy about things like that, especially anything to do with him. She wouldn't even mind his asking her at the last moment. Typical Jeff stuff, she'd say, and that would be that.

At home he followed his mother into her bedroom and watched her emptying the bureau, making stacks of clothes on the bed. 'Mom, I've got something to ask you.' Added a smile to make a mother's heart melt. Now that he was at the point of asking, he wasn't so sure his mother would be delighted with the arrangements he'd made. 'Mom, how are you feeling? Cheerful? You look great! You must be feeling good. You look like you're in your typical good mood. How would you like to have a baby in the house?'

'Love it, but not just yet,' his mother said. 'First let's get this marriage out of the way, and then the grandchildren.'

'I'm not talking about Natalie, Mom. Me.'

'You!' She stopped and looked at him. 'What are you planning now?'

'The plan is to have a baby visit us for a few days.'

'What baby? Whose baby?'

'Remember Mary? She's got that cute little baby you liked so much. She needs somebody to watch Hannah for a few days, and I said we'd do it.'

'We?'

'That's the royal we. I mean me. I'm going to do it. I just wanted to tell you there's going to be a baby in the house. You can be the supervisor. I'll be the nursemaid, change diapers, et cetera.'

'You, take care of a baby? Don't make me laugh.' She opened the closet door. 'Get me down that suitcase, will you? Why you?'

'Because Mary needs somebody she can trust.'

'Where's her mother?'

'In Florida with Mary's sick father.'

'No other relatives? Friends? Girlfriends? What about the Belcos? She said she was living there.'

'It's just a living arrangement,' he said.

'You mean the two of them are alone? Mary and the little girl?'

'You got it, Mom.'

His mother stopped packing. Her busy fingers were at rest. She looked at him closely. 'Well . . . I should understand what's going on, but I don't.'

'Try friendship.'

'I don't want to pry, but would you mind answering a simple question?'

He could read his mother's mind and searched for something reassuring to say. Something to put a mother's demons to rest. No, Mom, this isn't my baby. No, Mom, Mary and I aren't . . . I only wish we were . . . But that's another subject.

'No, Mom, Hannah is not—'

'And Mary?'

The conversation was turning into one of these fill-in-the-answer forms. 'Me and Mary? Not that, either. Not that I don't wish—'

She sat down on the bed. 'You know what they say – the wish is father to the deed.'

'Indeed! But in this case no deed, Mom. So, is it okay about Hannah?'

'I take it you promised already? Asking me is just a courtesy?'

He put his arm around her. 'Hey, Mom, you're going to help me out.'

'Don't I always? When's all this happening?'

'Mary's leaving day after tomorrow.'

'Day after tomorrow we're not going to be here, my absentminded son. Your father and I are leaving tomorrow morning for your sister's wedding.'

'What? Tomorrow morning?' Natalie's wedding. A little detail he'd let slip by him. He fell back on the bed, whimpering. They were going to the wedding. Leaving. His mother was leaving. Deserting him. 'You can't go.' All the starch was out of him. He had promised Mary, but it was always with the idea of his mother in the background. His mother hovering there, rescuing him, taking charge when things got too tough for him. He felt weak. 'Mom, I need you here. What am I going to do with a baby for four days?'

'I don't know. What are you going to do?'

He pulled a pillow over his face, screaming silently, tasting the days before him, panicking. Alone with Hannah for four days and four nights. Just Hannah and him. He couldn't do it. He knew he couldn't do it. What did he know about babies? As Mary had said, so he'd changed a diaper. Biiiig production. *Close-up:* Jeff changing Hannah. *Cut. Close-up:* Jeff holding Hannah. *Cut.* Mary overcome with gratitude.

'I can't do it, Mom.'

'Call her and say you can't do it, then. She'll just have to make other plans.'

'I can't do that, either.'

'Then you've got a problem, Jeff.'

He watched his mother fold one of his father's shirts into the suitcase, then roll up socks and underwear. Her fingers were so calm and competent. What did it matter to her (heartless, selfish mother) that he was having a break-down? He'd be drowning here and she'd be dancing at his sister's wedding. 'Can't Natalie change her wedding day? What difference does it make when they get married? They've been living together for three years. They can wait a few more days.'

'Now I've heard everything.'

'You're not going to help me, right? I can count on that!'

'Jeff—'

'Forget it!' He jumped up.

'What are you going to do?'

'Whatever I'm going to do, I'm going to do.'

The Belco line was busy. Maybe Mary was calling him. She'd had a change of heart all on her own, realized it was too much to ask him. It was wonderful that he'd offered, but she couldn't accept. Too much responsibility, but she'd never forget that he was ready to do it. He wouldn't be hurt, would her, because she didn't want to leave Hannah? She was so young – he understood, didn't he, that it wasn't good to leave little babies? Of course . . . of course.

He tried the number again. Still busy. Maybe she was calling the workshop, cancelling out. Good thinking, Mary. There'd be another workshop, next summer, and she'd be first in line. And he'd be better prepared, he'd do it then.

Danny finally answered the phone. 'Let me talk to Mary,' Jeff said.

'Jeff? You want me to get her? She's kicking a suitcase down the stairs. What's going on?'

Packed! Two days early. She wasn't going to let him off the hock. Not after she'd netted him. She wasn't cancelling. Not Mary. She was going to be the first one in line this summer! So eager she couldn't wait to dump Hannah on him. Oh, she was clever. *Let's ask Hannah . . . Last chance to back out.* Oh, sly woman. 'Put Mary on,' he said to Danny. 'I want to talk to her.'

She came on the phone a moment later. 'Jeff? Everything okay? Wait a second, I want to close the kitchen door.' She came back. 'I told Mrs. Belco Hannah and I are going away for the weekend, but she doesn't know where. I've got everything ready to bring over. It's almost all downstairs. Hannah's high chair and her food, extra bottles and baby oil and her playpen. I think I thought of everything. She can sleep in the playpen. Friday morning all I'll do is call the cab. So how about your mother? Is she looking forward to it?'

'Ah . . . ah . . .'

'Is she there? Can I talk to her?'

'Ah . . . ah . . .'

'Oh, never mind, don't bother her. I'm so excited. I can't believe I'm going—' She broke off, and he heard her saying to Danny, 'Don't touch anything, Danny, I'll take care of it.' She came back on the line. 'So I'll see you Friday morning?'

'Right, right . . . fine, fine . . . everything's fine.'

He didn't tell her, couldn't tell her. Just couldn't bring himself to disappoint her. Was it cowardice? Or was it love? What did it matter – it was going to be a disaster. What if Hannah woke at night and he didn't hear her? *Close-up:* Hannah shaking the bars of the playpen. *Cut to* Jeff asleep. *Cut to* Hannah frowning disapprovingly at Jeff (For four days.) *Cut to* Hannah in high chair, lips tight, refusing food. (For four days.) *Quick cuts:* Hannah crying in playpen. Hannah crying in high chair. Hannah crying in stroller. Hannah crying indoors. Hannah crying outdoors. (For four days!)

'You didn't tell her?' his mother said later. 'I don't know, Jeff. Maybe it'll be a good experience for you.' She sounded doubtful. 'Something like this will give you a taste of the real world. You do know where to reach Hannah's mother if you need her? And you have Natalie's number. We'll be there the day after tomorrow. You better have a whole list of emergency numbers, just in case. I suppose I shouldn't worry. You're eighteen. I know you can do it if you concentrate. Just remember you're dealing with a helpless human being.'

21

Hannah was crying, high piercing screams. She was sitting up on the couch, the pillows stacked around her. Mary had put her there when she arrived that morning. Hannah had been all smiles – smiles for her mother, smiles for Jeff. She had gone to sleep like a lamb. 'Put her in the playpen when she wakes up,' Mary had whispered, and she left. Then Hannah woke up and saw him, and that's when the screaming started.

With Hannah screaming, he couldn't think straight. The playpen refused to open. Hannah was red and rigid, furious. A dirty trick had been played on her. She hated him, hated his face, hated seeing him near her.

Those screams. Furious. Bloodcurdling. Bright red. Mouth gaping open. No letup, no weakening. Volume turned up full. Fortissimo. Where were all those screams coming from? How could a baby this size scream this long and this hard and this loud? She had the stamina of a marathon runner, the lungs of an opera singer. He clamped his hands over his ears. She was going to scream day and night for four days. Those screams were going to tear the roof right off the house. 'Shut up!' he whimpered.

She stopped in midscream, swivelled her head around to look at him, her eyes sticky and red with tears. Mary's smoky grey eyes looking at him accusingly. Where's my mother? What are you doing here? I don't like you!

'Tough luck, kid. You're stuck with me.' He could see her winding up again, and he warned her. 'Don't start again. If this is some kind of record you're trying to set, Hannah, you've done it. The Guinness people heard you all the way over in England. They've got your name in the record book.'

She was at it again, screaming, hiccuping, burping with

rage. Screams like the rasping of crows. Like fire trucks coming. Like jet engines. Freezing his blood, congealing his brain. The screams filled every room in the house, all the closets, perched on every lamp and corner. He slammed the windows down, dropped the blinds, pulled the drapes, every second expecting the neighbours to storm the house and break down the door.

He ran around the room like an idiot with his fingers in his ears, leaping like a kangaroo, then waving his arms like a conductor, calling, 'More, more, more . . . keep it up. Louder! Louder! The police are coming. Satisfied now? They're going to put you in a dog kennel and me in a loony bin.'

He fell in a heap at her feet. 'Are you hungry? Tell me, Master. Does the beast want to be fed? Speak to me – but softly. Your servant trembles before you.'

Jumping up, he checked Mary's instructions. Five pages of closely detailed notes. What to feed Hannah for breakfast, for lunch, for supper, and in between. 'She likes her mashed squash for breakfast and oatmeal at supper.' He checked the time. Too early for lunch, but milk was always appropriate. Mary had left him enough bottles for a year. The refrigerator was full of nothing but Hannah's food. When she opened her mouth, he stuck the bottle in. 'Here. Plug up that screaming hole.' For a moment it shut her up. She sucked rapidly, then she spat it out.

He held the bottle in front of her face. 'Do you know what this is? This is for you, moron. Milk isn't my idea, it's your mother's. Do you want to see?' He showed her Mary's instructions. 'It's all here in writing. What do you want, beer?' He tried to give her the bottle again, but she just turned her head away and screamed. 'You are a mean vicious little kid. You know what those screams of yours sound like? You ever been beaten with a club? That's the way it feels. Stop! Quit it! You stop or I leave.' He went to the door. 'I'm not kidding, kid.'

She stopped screaming to watch him.

'Ah! You're not stupid. You see where I am now? That's where your little game is going to get you. Scream one more time and you're minus one servant.'

The silence lasted fifteen seconds, just long enough for him to get his brains unscrambled. Fifteen seconds, then five seconds more. He was counting. And then she let him have it. The volcano exploded. Vesuvius! Pompeii! Mount Saint Helens! This was the biggest mistake of his life. He slapped himself in the face. 'So, so quick to say yes, yes . . . yes, Mary, yes! I adore you. I kiss your feet. Anything you want, Mary! Go away and leave me with Hannah? I'd love it. Yes, Mary. How come Hannah never screams like this when you're around?'

He wanted help. Mary, his mother, Mrs. Belco. Danny. Anybody! 'You see what you're doing to me, creep? Are you happy, enjoying yourself, having fun? I'm glad somebody's having a good time. Me? I'm leaving.'

He walked out on her, went to his room, turned his stereo on full, all out, and put on the earphones. Ah, the peace and quiet of rock. He sat back on the floor, hands behind his head, snapped his fingers, rolled his shoulders, shut his eyes. Drums . . . percussion . . . electric guitars . . . bass. Peace . . .

But there was no peace.

Great going, Jeff. Hiding in your room. Defeated by a baby.

I don't like war.

All you know how to do is talk.

What was he supposed to do? He gave her a bottle. He told her he wasn't going to listen to her screaming. Now it was her move.

Where's your imagination? Where's your brains? Where's your famous inventive, creative self, big-shot director? Get into a little problem and you quit.

He tore off the earphones and flung them aside. It was

116

silent. Too silent. No music. No screaming. 'Hannah? Hannah?' he called again.

She was on the floor in the living room, lying there like a floppy doll. She'd fallen off the couch. She was so still, so quiet. He was afraid to touch her.

He went down on his knees next to her. 'Hannah?' At least she was breathing. But then he got worried. Were those short little snorts normal? Those little puffs of breath? He crawled around her and listened on the other side. Her eyes were shut, her shirt bunched up under her back. Why was she lying on her head? Was that the way she slept normally? He didn't want to tamper with that silence – she could sleep till her mother came back – but was it real sleep? At least when she was screaming, he knew she was alive.

He'd never heard her breathe before. Was that the way babies did it, those wheezy sounds? His own breath didn't sound too normal to him either. He'd never paid so much attention to breathing in his life.

'Hannah?' he said again. He shook her a little. Her eyes opened. She could barely raise her lids, then they shut again.

She was sleeping. She must have worn herself out screaming. Okay, then sleep, baby, sleep. Sleep till your mother comes back. Every minute she slept was a moment's peace, brought him a minute closer to Mary's return.

He tiptoed into the kitchen, got out bread and cheese, humming under his breath. Sleep, baby, sleep . . . He dropped the knife, and right on cue, she was off and screaming again. He spread mustard on the bread and some lettuce. 'Just hold your horses,' he yelled, 'I'm here. I hear you. The whole neighbourhood hears you. For all I know your mother hears you. You're spoiled, you know that? You expect people to run every time you open your yap.' He started to take a bite out of his sandwich, but she had ruined his digestion.

'You're getting your way, little Hitler,' he said. He charged back into the living room, scooped her up and raced around the room with her. 'Like that? This make you happy? Thirty laps around the Orloff Speedway.'

She stopped crying and he slowed down. She hiccuped and jumped up and down in his arms. She wanted more. She was a speed freak. Every time he stopped, she protested. Up and back he ran, through every room, up the stairs and back down, up again, into the bathroom, turned on the lights, turned them off, turned them on, slid open the shower door, lifted the toilet seat, turned on the taps, and for a grand finale flushed the toilet. 'That's it, Hannah, that's the deluxe tour.'

She hiccuped and bounced in his arms. 'Now we do the kitchen.' He ran around the kitchen, opening and shutting the cupboard doors and grabbing a bite out of his sandwich. He could feel the wet through her diaper. Gross! This was really going to be a disgusting experience. What should he do now? Finish his sandwich or change her diaper? The way it smelled, he lost his appetite anyway.

He got the diaper bag and the Pamper box from the bedroom and looked around for a place to operate. Dr Orloff. The kitchen table? Too gross even for the doctor. Not the couch, either. He finally put her on the floor. He didn't look when he took off the dirty diaper. The last time he'd done this, it was just a wet diaper, and Mary was there and Hannah wasn't squirming and sliding around in it.

Before he had the nappy off, she got her foot in it, and then it was on her overalls. He had to start all over again, change her from the bottom up and the inside out, holding his nose all the time. 'That's your own fragrant self. You sure don't smell like a rose.' He opened all the windows and flushed the diaper down the toilet. 'If that clogs up, Hannah, you're paying.'

Then, back to the other end, it was feeding time again. Mashed liver and peas. He dipped into the jar, shoved the spoon in the general direction of her mouth. He didn't want to look. After he fed her, it was time to air her. He'd promised Mary he'd get her outside every day.

He didn't have a minute to himself until she took her afternoon nap. This time he got the playpen open and put her in there. 'Now sleep,' he said and went into the kitchen. There was half a pizza in the freezer that he threw in the oven. He stepped out on the back porch. It was a great day. He wondered how long she'd sleep this time. She was safe in there. He lay down on the grass. A few minutes for himself. How'm I doing, Mary? You must be there by now. Thinking of me?

What would he do this afternoon? What could he do? Nothing. But still, if he could, what would he do? So much of his life lately had been focused around Mary, and now she wasn't here. Vague thoughts of California drifted through his mind – sun and beaches, movie sets, cameras, girls in yellow bikinis.

He smelled the pizza burning. His nose brought him the news. Then the phone rang. He ran inside and he lunged for it, got it before the second ring. It was Danny, looking for company. 'I'm going out to the lake for a swim.'

'Can't.'

'Why not?'

'Busy.'

'I thought while Mary was away you'd have some time for your friends. What're you doing?'

'Nothing.'

If he told him he was nursemaiding Mary's baby, Danny would say she had him wound around her little finger.

'I'll pick you up in fifteen minutes.'

He pulled the cord around so he could check on Hannah. 'I've got a friend over.'

'Bring him along.'

'Her. And she's sleeping over.'

'Somebody I know?'

'Mmmm . . .'

'Where are your folks?'

'They went away. They'll be gone for ten days.'

'Where'd you meet her? Has she got a friend?'

'I don't think you'd like her or her friends. They're all a bunch of slobs.'

'Well, she's hanging out with you, what do you expect?'

'Right now she's sleeping on the living room floor. When she wakes up, we're going to be taking a bath together.'

Danny whistled. 'Why don't you let me talk to her at least?'

'What about Tracy?'

Danny was silent for a moment. 'We had a big fight. We're not seeing each other right now.'

'That sounds serious. How come?'

'You know . . . we just don't agree.'

When Jeff got off the phone, the female in his life was standing up in the playpen, her diaper at half mast, looking miserable and mean, her lip trembling. When she saw him she raised her arms, and he scooped her up. 'You wanted to talk to Danny? I didn't think so. But if he calls again, I'll put you on. Then you blast him. High C.' He was feeling okay till he checked her diaper and there it was again. Another special delivery package!

This time he changed her fast – too fast. Whipped the diaper off, whisked another one on. She didn't like it and started to complain. You're pretty rough on me. He picked her up. 'Listen, I'm sorry. This is my first day, Hannah. I'm new on the job.'

For the rest of the day, he hauled her around everywhere. He hung out with her. Fed her again, gave her a bottle, changed her. Cleaned her up for bed. He walked her until she fell asleep in his arms, then sat with her, watching TV, afraid to put her down. He was wiped out. The house looked like a hurricane had come into the front door and stayed for the weekend. And this was only the first day, he reminded himself. It was just the beginning.

22

Jeff woke to Hannah's babbling. He'd slept on the couch. She was talking to her foot in the playpen. He wasn't sure, but the foot might have been answering back. He was still groggy from watching late TV and could have used some more sleep, but there was no sleep with Hannah awake. He lay there, chin on his hand, watching her. In his head, behing his eyes, a story unfolded, a screenplay for a movie about a guy living by himself, no family, no friends, who gets this baby thrust on him. A woman he meets on the street leaves it with him. He holds the kid for her as a favour, and then she disappears and he, poor sap, is stuck with this brat he doesn't want.

Not a happy scenario. It was Mary he was thinking about, and now he wasn't dreaming about her returning filled with gratitude, love, and lust. How did he know she was coming back at all? Maybe she'd set this whole thing up to get rid of her kid. There was a guy she was meeting. The son of Someone Famous! They'd planned it for a long time, just waiting for the right patsy to appear. Jeff Orloff met all the requirements. Gullible, dependable, eager to please, softhearted. Softheaded. He looked at Hannah with dread. Was she his forever?

And when his parents came home, what then? Maybe they'd let him stay, but not for long. They weren't going to take care of Hannah. One of his father's favourite sayings was. You got yourself into this mess, now get yourself out.

Good-bye California, good-bye freedom, good-bye everything.

Meanwhile Hannah was trying to get her foot in her mouth. No screams this morning, no red, squeezed face. Too busy chewing on her foot. She was already used to him. He was old hat. She'd probably forgotten her mother, too. What did she care who the nurse was as long as she had service twenty-four hours a day?

He tried a fast one, threw her a biscuit in the playpen, then tried to sneak away to the bathroom. Up went the siren and he came running back. Twenty-four hours, and she had him trained.

'The reason you don't talk,' he told her in the bathroom, 'is because you've got your staff so terrorized they do anything you want before you want it.'

For breakfast he put her in the walker. Half of what he gave her she sprayed over the floor. 'Who's going to clean that up? Not you, creeper.' He put her down on the floor. 'Here, have a feast.' She went crawling away, mumbling to herself. She was like a goat, everything went into her mouth. She tried out the leg of the chair, the edge of the coffee table, his sneakers. It was a full-time job just keeping her from poisoning herself. She was in the cupboards, the pots, the brooms, the stack of old newspapers, exploring everything with her fingers and her mouth. He hauled her out from under the sink and shoved a chair against it, then gave her a hunk of melon to gnaw on.

He liked to eat a leisurely breakfast in the morning. He considered this the most important meal of the day, but there was no settling down. When he tried to keep Hannah in the kitchen, she howled. Ditto the playpen. So he let her roam free, ran to the kitchen, grabbed something to eat and ran back to check her.

'Hey, rug rat, you think I'm going to chase after you all day?' But that was exactly what he did. He closed doors, barricaded the staircase, and waited for her to get tired and fall asleep. Then he was going to make some calls. He had friends to talk to – he hadn't spoken to an intelligent human being since Hannah arrived.

'Why don't you sleep?' he suggested. As far as he was concerned, that was the only appealing thing that babies did. He tried to put her in the playpen again, but she wasn't buying. He spread her blanket on the rug and pushed her head down. She kept bobbing up. Finally he lay down beside her. 'Watch me. Stop kicking, hold the legs straight.' He demonstrated. 'If I can make a suggestion – see how comfortable Jeff is. Now you do it.'

He had to straighten her out a couple dozen times, but she finally settled down, hanging on to his finger. 'Don't scream in my ear and we'll get along – I don't say we're going to be best friends. Now close your eyes, like this. Do the way I do.'

He shut his eyes, then opened them. She was sitting up again. He pushed her down. She bobbed up. 'Down. Shut those eyes. When I shut mine, you shut yours.' This time he didn't open his eyes. 'Breathe the way I'm breathing. You doing it, Hannah?' He peeked. She'd turned over, was lying flat on her stomach, arms sprawled out, making little sleepy pig sounds. He told himself to get up, but he lay there listening to the regular rise and fall of her breath and fell asleep himself.

When he woke up, she was gone. 'Hannah!' He flew through the house, looking behind the doors and under the beds, his head a spider's nest of horrors. Had she somehow got out of the house? What if she'd flushed herself down the toilet! He found her in the closet in his parents' room, on the floor, buried under his mother's long bathrobe. She'd pulled it down on herself. 'You little idiot, what are you so happy about? You could have smothered yourself.'

He got so nervous about the house and all the ways it could poison, choke, and strangle her that he took her outside. It was hot. He was wearing shorts and sandals, Hannah was strapped in her chestpack. Hannah's sack, with all the emergency supplies, was over his shoulder, like they were going on an expedition to Mount Everest.

Carrying her on his chest, he felt like a nursing mother, so he put her on his shoulders. More masculine image. She grabbed his hair and his ears. Holding the reins of a horse. Beat her feet against his chest. Giddyap. 'Where to, boss? You want to go anyplace special? How about the movies?'

Genius thought. It was cool in the theatre, Hannah in his lap sucking on her bottle. She cosied right down with it. Actually slept. But when she woke up, he had to leave because she was jumping around. Outside, it was hot, so they trekked over to the Mall, looking for shelter.

He wedged her between his feet while he played Pac-Man and Space Invaders. 'Sit right there, road rat.' But then he got caught up in the game, and when he looked she was crawling toward the door.

He scooped her under his arm and walked around with her. He was getting lots of long, friendly, warm looks from women. It would have been nothing to start up a conversation. Babies and dogs were surefire.

He bought frozen yogurt cones and sat down with her. She promptly dropped her cone on the floor. She made a dive for it, but he clamped her between his legs and gave her his. He was having a good time watching the couples going by, the girls with their arms around their guys, fingers through their belt loops or in their back pockets. One of these days Mary and he were going to be like that. The happy scenario again.

Christopher Columbus got away from him, crawled a little way, turned around to check him out, then came back. She banged on his knees and took off again, grabbing on to a woman's leg. A jogger, judging from the outfit she was wearing.

'Your little girl thinks she knows me,' the jogger said, bringing Hannah back. 'She's beautiful. How old is she?'

'About a year, I think. Or maybe it's two. How old does she look to you?'

'You don't know your own daughter's age?'

'You want her?' he said. 'She's on special today.'

The woman gave him a peculiar look and walked away, then hung around the Orange Julius stand a long time, watching him.

He let Hannah go again. She was like bait on a fishing line. This time she caught an old man, dressed up with a tie and jacket. He was talking to her and leading her back slowly. 'I found her for you.' He sat down and started telling Jeff about his grandchildren. They all lived someplace else. He saw them, but not often. He lived alone, like Jeff's grandfather, and came over here to the Mall every afternoon. 'They take your blood pressure here and there's always somebody to talk to. First time I've seen you. Do you work nights?'

He pointed to Hannah. 'She's my job.'

'You're one of those house fathers. Your wife works. That's becoming more common. There was a TV programme about that on the Donahue show. Father stays home with junior and mother brings home the paycheque. I couldn't do that.

'I used to be a railway conductor. Forty years for the New York Central. I bet you thought passenger trains. Nope, freights. You know what a caboose is?'

It was steamy when they left the Mall. He carried Hannah in his arms. For a while he considered going up to the park and both of them dunking in the pool to cool off, but it was getting late, and according to Mary's schedule, this was bathtime, dinnertime, and bedtime. 'It's your time all the time, chief.'

Hannah was fretful, complaining, pounding him with her feet. 'Listen, the heat's not my fault. What do you want me to do?' He fanned her with a newspaper. 'Why don't you answer me? I talk to you all the time, and you never say an intelligent word. Say "Jeff," ' he instructed her. Maybe he'd get her to talk before Mary came back. That would impress Mary. 'Jeff, that's easy. Four letters. Say something. Stop mooing. No, I don't want you to say "mama." Any moron can say that. Say something else, your conversation is getting boring. Say "yes." Say "no." We're down to two-letter words.' He took her chin in his hand. 'Look at me, kid. See the way I do it.' He puckered his lips. '*Noooo*.' Then stretched his mouth. '*Yeesss*.' She poked her fingers in his eyes. 'You're hopeless,' he said.

At home, it was too hot to face the gross mess inside, so he filled Hannah's pink plastic tub on the patio. He threw in a steamboat, a rubber ball, and a plastic duck. He took off her clothes and put her in. She had a great time slapping the water and throwing the toys out so Jeff could fetch them. 'How about inviting me into your swimming pool? No? Well, here I come.' He kicked off his sandals and stuck his feet in. She grabbed for them. A new toy.

He gave her supper in the tub. That was innovative. Easier to clean her afterward. Everything ended up in the water – mashed baby beef and carrots and apricot sauce for dessert. He was feeding her out of three jars first, but she was so slow he finally mixed everything together. It all ended up in the same place, didn't it? 'That's the way, oink, oink, oink – good little pig.'

He was ready with the next spoonful before she'd swallowed the first one. 'Come on, open up, garbage mouth.' He pushed the spoon against her mouth. 'Open the barn door. Here comes the wagon. You want to see me do it?' He tried a spoonful and gagged. 'Now that's delicious! Your turn, Hannah.' She opened her mouth, and the mess oozed out and ran down her chest and into the water.

She protested when he pulled her out of the pool, complained when he cleaned her up, got all twisted up in her pyjamas, bawled when he put her in the playpen, but finally took the bottle in both mitts and fell asleep sucking it. End of Day Two. Two down and two to go.

23

There was a routine to taking care of a baby, a way to do things. It helped if you could do two things at once. Required equipment for prospective mothers and babysitters: an extra pair of arms and a double order of hands and fingers. By the third day, Jeff was an expert. He could change her diaper, warm her bottle, and talk to her all at once.

'Good morning, Hannah. How are you this morning? Remember me? I'm the one you pee on.' He checked her. 'Yep. No surprises. Right on schedule. You put UPS to shame. Watch this, kid.' He put one hand behind his back and changed her diaper. 'You see, peepot, no matter how inept you are at the beginning, you can learn.' Not that he was going to hang out his shingle, because no money in the world could pay for the abuse he took. This queen wanted total, complete, and undivided attention. And anything Her Majesty wanted, Her Majesty got.

'You've got me pinned under your big little thumb. I don't know how you did it. I'm bigger than you are, stronger, taller, tougher. I can push you over with the tip of my little finger.' He demonstrated, pushed her over. 'You see, pipsqueak, might makes right. But you, squirt, you don't play by the rules. Who else commands with a grunt? How did you figure that one out? Grunter, you're a genius and you're not even a year old.'

As he talked, he changed her, his fingers did the work. Undershirt dry. 'How'd you miss that, Miss Pee-in-the-Ocean?' Leave the undershirt on. Don't touch anything that doesn't have to be touched till after morning pig-time.

He emptied her squash into the tray in front of her. She ate the way she talked, without regard for order, tradition, good manners. She talked all the time. At first he'd thought it was nonsense, no sense, babbling, but he'd changed his mind about that. It wasn't babbling. It was her language. Real talk. Her own words. Sometimes her words even sounded like everyone else's language. As for the way she ate, that was individual, too.

She pushed the food into her mouth with her fingers, hands, elbows. She had mashed-whatever in her hair and on her chin and up her nose. 'Enjoying yourself? Your mother wouldn't let you eat this way, but I do. Eat what you want the way you want to.' She was too busy mouthing her squash to answer. 'You know what it is that makes people happy, baby? Doing what you want to, the way you want to, when you want to, and no comments.'

He fed her seedless grapes one at a time. 'One more day and then you-know-who will be back. I'm not mentioning any names because I don't want you bawling on me again. You miss her, don't you? Same here, but don't tell her that.'

He offered her another grape. She shook her head. 'I'm like you. A man of few words. Some things don't have to be said. Some things, the less said the better. You like somebody, you don't have to be saying "I like you" all the time. You begin to sound like everyone else and people think you're not sincere. Act like you like them and they know you like them. But you know that better than I do. Everybody likes you. You're in perfect harmony with your world, Mighty Mouse. That's why you're a genius.'

He peeled a banana on her tray. 'What do you think you-know-who is going to say when she comes back and sees how you've thrived and matured? She'll be impressed, right? You bet she will be. Everything's going to take on a different colour, a different perspective, do you know what I mean, peewee? You can be too close to people, take them for granted, but step back, squint through your other eye, and you get another angle, a fresh perspective. And who's going to be in the centre of that eye? Not you, me. Get it?

It's going to be one hell of a reunion. There may not be a lot of talk, but the feeling between us is going to be intense.

'What are you laughing about? You think you're the only one she's interested in. Well, you happen to be wrong. Four days away from me and she isn't going to be able to keep her hands off me. Don't snicker, droolface. What do you know about it? You're an expert on how to be a baby, but when it comes to men and women you've got a lot to learn. Think you're the only expert on feelings? You do what you feel like doing, right? I do, too, and right now I feel like rubbing some banana right into your fat little face.'

After Hannah finished eating, he dressed her, diaper, shorts, sleeveless shirt. He had to change, too. Standard operating procedure after every meal. The dirty stuff he kicked in the corner, the dishes he stacked in the sink. Save everything for the last day when there would be a monster neighbourhood bazaar and cleanup.

'Kid, what do we do today? I feel weird being alone with you all the time. It feels like I've been stuck with you forever. What if I *was* stuck with you? What if it was a world where men got pregnant and you were mine to have or not to have? I don't know if you'd be here. Get that pout off your face, blubber mouth. I'm just talking. You're safe. You're here, aren't you?

'Maybe it's a good thing men don't get pregnant. We're too selfish to have babies. I am, anyway. I don't vision myself hauling a watermelon around under my belt for nine months. What happens if I don't feel like carrying you around every minute? Do I leave you at the baggage check-in?

'Remember, I don't know it's you yet, and I'm thinking what a sap I am giving you this free ride. Now, in a just world, pregnant women – pardon me, pregnant persons – would have time off for good behaviour, check out of the scene when it got to be too much.

'What do you weigh inside there? Twenty-five pounds?

Thirty pounds? Who needs it? You're smiling now because you know if you ever got in there, I'd be stuck, and once you got out, I'd be stuck forever. Mother Jeff.

'We pregnant men don't take to being full-time porters and freight carriers. Everywhere I go, you'd go? Everything I eat, you eat? If you don't like my food, I get the bellyache? What if I don't want you eating my food? I don't! I don't want you inside my belly. I don't want you rooting around in there, burping and farting and pissing. Sitting in there with that smug smile on your face 'cause you got me. No way. Get out! Get out and take care of yourself! Nine months! Too much. I have too many other things to do with my life. What am I going to do with you in California? I'm looking for work in the industry and there I am, pregnant with you! Oh, you're pregnant, they'll say. You can't work. You've got your job right inside you. Go home and take care of your brat.

'Hannah, the smartest thing you ever did was pick Mary for your mother. You were smart before you were born. If you'd picked me, you might not have been so lucky. You might not even be here. Sorry about that. The truth is I wouldn't have known it was you, till it was you. I admit you're neat to have around – sometimes. Mostly when you're sleeping. And if I was alone, I can see that you'd be someone to talk to. Except that I'd only be alone because I'd be stuck with you. If I was alone on an island with a dog, I'd be talking to him, too, after three days.

'It feels like I haven't talked to a human being in three months.' He put her on his back, grabbed her sack. 'You don't believe any of this stuff. You think I talk too much, don't you? Or do you just think, Let him talk, let him blab on, in the end I'll have my own way?'

Outside the heat pushed into his face. 'Where to today, boss? It's too hot to be walking around. You want to go to the park? Yeah? Let's go swimming. Yeah? You say yeah to everything. You're a good kid. We're going swimming.

Now if you'd only learn how to talk and throw a ball and use the toilet you'd be some fun to be with.'

24

Day Four. The last day. The day Mary came back. 'Let's get this show on the road, Hannah. We don't want to be slipshod today. We get out early, beat the heat, have our swim, and get back in time to get everything in place for you-know-who.'

At the wading pool there was a screaming mess of kids knocking into each other and thrashing through the water. It was a dangerous place for a little kid. He kept Hannah to one side where she wouldn't be trampled. The benches were lined with watching mothers, plus a few token fathers. One bearded dude in a Mickey Mouse shirt nodded to Jeff. He nodded back and smiled at the mothers, too.

Hannah brought the water to her face and it ran between her fingers. Then she let the water run down her arms. The floppy hat he set on her head kept falling off. Her little shirt got drenched and he pulled it off. She was the only kid in the pool with a diaper on. The rest wore slick little nylon swimsuits and bikinis. 'But what have you got to hide, peewee? No use sticking out your chest yet, but don't worry – if you're anything like your mother, you're going to have what it takes.'

He couldn't shake the feeling the mothers were watching him. One mother in particular, small and wiry, with glasses, the type who carried a whistle on a string around her neck. The mothers on that bench were all professionals with their carriages and trikes and toys, but she looked like the most professional of all. The old pro looking over the new boy.

Hannah kept getting up and falling in the water. Her diaper drooped and he pulled it up. It finally fell down for keeps and he took it off. What was wrong with a little kid running around naked? Even if she peed a little in the water, as long as no one drank it . . .

The skinny woman barked out an order. 'Ron, slow down!' A big kid with his hair plastered over his forehead froze, then took off after his friends again. Jeff had noticed Ron before. He had big feet and the loudest voice in the pool.

'Ron! I said slow down!'

The kid threw himself over backwards and almost fell on Hannah. Jeff thrust him aside. 'Watch it, Ron!'

The next thing he knew Ron's mother was at the edge of the pool, ready to kill. 'Don't you shove my kid around, mister. Just keep your big paws to yourself. That pool doesn't belong to you or your kid, either. This is a public pool. And she's not supposed to be in here with her clothes off.'

'Where does it say that?'

'Where does it say that? Very good, very clever. Is that the way you talk to your pals? Pull that smart stuff on me and I'll have you out of here so fast your head will spin.' She marched back to the bench.

'What's that all about?' he whispered to Hannah. 'That lady's crazy. That's the way some people get their jollies, water rat. There's a lesson here for you about life, but I don't know if you'll appreciate knowing it so young.'

He kept his back to the women's bench. He was sure Ron's mother was talking about him, and in his head he was answering back. She didn't intimidate him. He wasn't leaving because of her. But he finally did just that, hauled Hannah, protesting and slapping him on the face, out of the water. I don't want to leave yet. I'm having fun. Just because Ron's mother yelled a little.

He dressed her on the concrete wall. 'Come on, you pill, it's time to go anyway. She didn't drive me away. Remember who's coming today?' He checked his watch. It was earlier than he thought. Time was dragging. 'She won't be here for a while, Hannah, but she's on her way right now.'

Reunion. The meeting of Jeff and Mary . . . the moment when they'd see each other . . . fly toward each other . . .

'What are you going to do when you see her? You going to cry? Are you going to laugh? Maybe a little of both, right? And maybe you'll act like she never went away. Cool cat. It hasn't been bad, has it?'

Hannah pinched his nose.

'Okay, I admit I was a little rough in the beginning. Are you going to say something to her about that?'

She pinched it again.

'You are! You fink.' He picked her up and put her on his shoulders. 'After all, I didn't really know what a baby was before. Four days with you, Hannah, and my whole perspective has changed. You want to know how, Teach? Your mother can't do anything with you hanging on her back. Taking care of you is a full-time job. She needs me. She needed me to get away. And she's going to need me when she comes back. What do you think about me being around all the time?'

He craned his neck to look up at her. 'You like that, huh? I'm not sure about every minute. We won't necessarily live together, that still has to be negotiated, but we're going to be really close. She wants to be an actress. I want to be a director. It's a natural for us to help each other. I'm an expert on you now. With me around she'll have more time for herself. And for me.'

Long shot: Mary approaching the Orloff house. *Close-up:* Mary's face full of anticipation. *Reverse shot:* Jeff out front holding up Hannah. *Long shot:* Mary running. *Close on* the three of them embracing, Mary kissing the baby (*sound of violins*). *Close-up:* Mary, with tears in her eyes. Oh my darling, I couldn't stop thinking about you the whole time I was away. It's been torture. I couldn't wait to get back. *Another angle:* Jeff kissing Mary. *Fade out.*

Hannah had a stranglehold on his neck. He whipped her around into his arms. 'Oh, my darling.' He held her up in front of him and kissed her neck passionately. She squealed and blew spit bubbles into his face.

'You like that? You got to be careful who you kiss. I don't want you kissing every man who's nice to you.' He sat down near the slides with Hannah in his lap and whispered into her ear, 'This is between you and me. Mary is my inspiration.'

He took Hannah over to the big kids' slide. She had to wait for her turn. Then he put her on halfway up and caught her at the bottom. They'd done it four or five times when Big Foot Ron came flying over the top and knocked Hannah off the slide.

Jeff snatched her up. For a second, she was speechless. 'Hannah, are you okay?' She started to whimper. Her cheek was scraped. He brushed away the dirt, and she jerked away and started bawling.

Ron's mother came over. 'What happened?'

'Your kid!' Jeff said in a sudden rage. 'He knocked her off the slide.'

'Ron, get over here, you big jerk.' She grabbed her kid. 'You see what you did to that poor baby?'

He carried Hannah home in his arms. She was trembling and choking on her sobs. A woman on the street said, 'Oh, poor baby. Take her in to the druggist. He'll give you something.' In the drugstore, the pharmacist looked at Hannah's cheek. 'Just a skin burn,' she said and recommended a healing, soothing cream. Jeff put some on right away and she quietened down.

He'd been dreaming about the reunion with Mary. Some reunion. Mary would take one look at Hannah's cheek and God knows what she'd think. Child abuse.

'She might have a little tolerance, Hannah. After all, I'm not your father. I never had a kid sister. I'm the baby in my family. You didn't know that, did you, Hannah? But if you think about it, you'll realize that's why I don't treat you like a baby.'

At home he put more cream on the bruise, cooling it with his breath. 'Feeling better? You're a brave little shit. You didn't cry a lot.'

When it was time to eat, the only thing she wanted was her bottle with juice. Jeff lay down on the floor with his face next to hers and looked into her eyes the way he couldn't look into anyone else's eyes. She looked back at him, her eyes wide, unblinking, with a trusting open look that went deep inside him. It hurt to look at her. Love was what he saw in her eyes. It scared him. A few days ago, he'd hardly known she existed and now – when had it happened? – he was caught.

25

Later that day, the phone rang. 'Jeff?' Mary said. 'It's me. How's Hannah?'

'She's fine. Where are you? Are you here?'

She hesitated. 'I'm—I'm—Well, I hope you don't mind, but I won't be coming back until tomorrow morning.'

'Tomorrow morning?'

'Can you hang on one more night? The reason I didn't call sooner is that I've been incredibly busy. I'll definitely be there tomorrow morning. Do you think your mother would mind?'

'My mother—' He coughed. He'd forgotten that Mary thought his mother was there, backing him up.

She caught something in his voice right away. 'What's going on, Jeff? Are you sure Hannah is okay?'

'Mary, my mother's not here. She hasn't been here the whole time. She's in Washington at my sister's wedding.'

'It's just you and Hannah?'

'Yes. But everything's been fine. Hannah and I are having a great time.'

'You distinctly told me your mother would be there. I would never have left Hannah with you alone.'

'Thanks for your vote of confidence. What do you think happened? Nothing until today.'

'Today?'

'It's nothing.'

'What's nothing? Jeff, you're making me crazy.'

'Everything's fine, Mary. Don't get excited, it's just a scrape. Some jerky kid knocked her down in the playground and she scraped her cheek. I put something on it, a cream I got at the drugstore.'

'Are you sure she's okay, Jeff?'

'She's sleeping like a lamb.'

'At four o'clock? She won't be able to sleep tonight.'

'Oh, yes she will.' He felt he knew more about Hannah than she did. He was with Hannah, not her. 'Hey wait – she's waking up right now. Do you want to talk to her?'

He brought Hannah to the phone. 'Say hello to your mother, Hannah.'

Right on cue, she started babbling.

'Hello, sweetie!' Mary said. 'Hello, baby. Hello little face. I miss you, honey. Mommy's coming home soon.'

'Oh, Hannah,' he said, the next morning, as they sat eating breakfast together in the living room. She was in her walker. He was barefoot, in gym shorts. The TV was on, but neither of them was watching. 'Mary's coming home today. You're thrilled, aren't you, Hannah?'

'Raraa,' she said.

'That's right. Your mother. You're a smart little slob. Is Mary going to be happy to see us, Hannah, is she going to be impressed? Here you are, feeding yourself and look at the way we're talking. I wonder if your mother is aware that even though you don't say a lot, you understand everything.'

'Rye rye rye,' Hannah agreed.

'Right. It's been good for you to be with me, Hannah. You need a man around. Mothers worry about everything. Men are more relaxed. They take things as they come.' Then he thought of his own parents. 'Well, not in every case. But enough of this for now. This is the plan. We're going to be cleaned up and waiting when Mary walks in that door.'

They walked around, surveying the house. 'Can you believe it, Hannah? How can one kid do this. We ought to apply for Federal Disaster Aid.'

The couch pillows were on the floor, the chairs were turned backwards, there were toys everywhere and a wet diaper on the rug. Even the pictures on the walls were crooked. He tossed the pillows back into place, then the chairs, then all the toys into the corner and the diaper into the garbage.

The kitchen was worse. The table was invisible. He dropped an empty granola box and a pile of carrot scrapings into the trash. 'Hannah, I'll take a little credit for this.' He filled the sink with soapy water and started the dishes soaking, then grabbed a bunch of half empty boxes and shoved them back in the cupboard. Then he went through the house like a Camaro, Hannah wheeling after him in her walker. Later, he lay on the floor, his feet up on the couch. Hannah crawled to the window and stood up, talking to herself.

'See your mother yet? Pretty soon.'

They waited for her all morning, not going anywhere or doing anything for fear of missing her. At noontime he and Hannah ran out to the market to buy some last-minute things Mary would like, Heavenly Hash ice cream, canned peaches, and chocolate-covered graham crackers. Then a bunch of things for himself that he never ate, but this was special. They were going to have a party.

All day he waited for Mary, tied to the house, tied to the clock. He expected her every minute, kept looking up, 'hearing' her, running out to check. By the middle of the afternoon he was steaming. What was she pulling on him? What was her excuse? Was he going to get another phone call?

He threw her instructions away and fed Hannah anything she wanted. She chewed on his pizza, took a swig of his beer, and shared his chocolate bar. Then he and Hannah sat together, watching TV. After waiting for Mary all day, he wasn't in the mood to get her ready for bed or even clean her up. Or himself, either.

'Jeff?'

It was late and dark, and he didn't hear her until she

was at the door. Then he nearly maimed himself getting his feet untangled. Mary! Finally! He took a swipe at the ring of yellow around Hannah's mouth and ran to the hall.

Mary, wearing shorts, a knapsack on her back, her braided hair in a crown on her head. She looked like a Tyrolean hiker asking for directions. 'You're early,' he said. Sarcasm right away. This wasn't the way he had imagined greeting her. This was The Reunion (*Music under – guitars strumming*). Mary and Jeff fall into each other's arms.

Instead, here he was in a pair of grubby shorts, a rag in one hand and Hannah in his arms, starting one of her world-famous arias.

And Mary – taller than he remembered her, face longer. Had she always had that space between her front teeth? Could four days make that much difference? 'Jeff!' She smiled, then reached for Hannah with a needy, wanting, hungry look.

He stood there waiting his turn. 'We've been waiting for you all day.'

'You sweet face.' Mary kissed Hannah, kissed the bruise on her cheek, kissed her hands, the backs and the palms, and each finger.

How about him? He put his arm around Mary and found himself patting her knapsack. He finally got his hands on her and rubbed her shoulder. 'Hey, Mary, it's great to see you again.'

'You, too, Jeff.'

26

'What a day it's been,' Mary said. 'I've been up since five-thirty this morning.' She hugged Hannah. 'It's so good to hold her again!' She smiled at Jeff. 'She really looks wonderful.'

He perched on the arm of her chair, his hand on her shoulder. 'I thought you were coming in the morning.'

'I thought so, too. I'm sorry, Jeff, but it was hard to get away. There were so many last-minute things to do. So many people to say good-bye to. I wish I could tell you everything that happened.'

'Why don't we just sit back and talk?' he said.

She stood up. 'I'm afraid if I relax I'll never get up again.' She picked up Hannah's sneakers. 'I ought to get going. Is all this stuff Hannah's? I've forgotten how much junk she has. Where do I start? What do I have to take with me? I should get back to the Belcos' before it's too late.'

'Why do you have to go tonight?' *Close-up:* Jeff's bed. Two heads. 'You can sleep here,' the hypocrite said. 'Lots of room.'

'No, Jeff, you don't want another night and morning of Hannah.'

'I don't mind. You're so tired . . . I'll put Hannah to bed. You just sit and watch me do my stuff.'

He cleaned out the playpen and put the sheet down. 'Usually she's asleep earlier, but I let her stay up for you. I sleep here on the couch to keep an eye on her.'

'That's where I'll sleep, then.'

So she was staying. 'That's great. We can sleep in here together.'

She caught his chin and smiled at him. 'Oh, no, you don't, Jeffy. I know where your mind is.'

'I just thought – in case she wakes up and you don't hear her.' He ruined it by smiling too happily.

'I'll help you clean up in the morning,' she said.

Mary put Hannah in the playpen, then sat down next to her, stroking her back. 'I'd like to crawl in the playpen and sleep with her.'

'We can hear her out in back.'

'I'll stay until she falls asleep. You go on out, Jeff. I'll be right with you.'

I'll be right with you. Very good. Once Hannah was asleep . . . He went outside, but he was back almost immediately.

'Shh . . .' Mary stood up, and they tiptoed out together. 'Poor thing finally gave up,' Mary said. In back, they sat down at the picnic table and she started telling him about the workshop. 'That first day I thought I'd made a terrible mistake. I missed Hannah so much. And I didn't know anybody. I almost turned around and came back, but by the end of the day I'd met Marsha. And that changed everything. I made a friend. Jeff, it was beautiful in the mountains. You would have loved it. Cool enough for blankets every night. We slept out a lot, the whole company, at the edge of the lake.'

Who slept with who? Everybody knew the mountains made you horny. 'We can sleep out, too,' he said.

'No, I wouldn't leave Hannah tonight. It would be terrible if she woke up and I wasn't there. She'd really feel betrayed.'

'So it was good?'

'It was wonderful! Getting away really gave me perspective.' She leaned toward him and took his hand. 'Do you remember how discouraged I was? I was so sure that I would never act again.'

He smoothed her skin, then cradled her arm in his.

'I was wrong about that. And I found out there's a way for people to help each other. Family, but not the old-style family. A new kind. A family of friends, people who come together because they have something in common.'

'That's exactly my idea. You know what I discovered these last few days? I like kids. I sure like Hannah.'

'And she likes you. I could see that right away.'

'And I agree with you about the family,' he said. 'We have to do things our own way, not the way our parents did it.'

'That's it,' she said.

He was singing inside. They were talking the same language. Their talk was like a staircase that took them higher and higher . . . and brought them closer and closer. 'Let me get you something to eat,' he said. 'I bought you great junk food.'

'I haven't pigged out since I left.'

He brought her a bowl of ice cream. 'Hannah's still sleeping.' He sat down close to her. 'You know, you've changed. Just these few days. You're more self-possessed and confident.'

'It was good for me to get away.'

It was stuffy when they went back in the house. They tiptoed around Hannah's playpen. He found a couple of sheets and a pillow for Mary. 'No blanket,' she said. 'It's too hot for that.'

'You all set?' He sat down on the edge of the couch. He waited . . . suspended in midair. Tomorrow she was going back to the Belcos'. It was now that it had to happen. They'd never have a better chance. 'You want anything else?'

'No, this is really fine.' She yawned a couple of times. 'Thanks, Jeff, for everything. Did I thank you? I should have!' She leaned over and kissed him on the cheek. 'I can't thank you enough. I would never have gone if you hadn't pushed me. I'll never forget that.'

And then she yawned and yawned again and again,

terrible yawns. 'I'm sorry, Jeff,' she said, covering her mouth. 'I just can't keep my eyes open.'

He went to his room but left the door open and lay awake, wishing she would come. It would be like that old movie, *The King of Hearts*, where Alan Bates slept and the beautiful tightrope walker crept into his room, leaned over his bed, and began kissing him . . .

He fell asleep, woke, and slept again. In a dream, he heard her calling him. He sat up like a shot. The dark square of the doorway and the hall it framed were empty. 'Mary?' He tiptoed to the living room. She was curled up on the couch, wrapped in the sheet, her head jammed into the pillow. Only her arm was sticking out, pointed straight at him.

'Mary?' If her arm moved, that was the signal.

He waited. It was so still in the house. Even the street was still. Nothing moved. The solitary car that passed seemed to gather the darkness to it. Hannah murmured in her sleep.

He squatted down. Mary's hand almost touched his knee. If he moved just slightly forward, they'd touch. And then she'd open her eyes . . .

Hannah tossed in the playpen. Jeff leaned forward and touched his lips to Mary's fingertips. There was a tremor in her hand, and he felt her fingers brush his cheek. And he saw everything . . . the way her arms would reach out and encircle him and pull him to her . . .

He waited . . . waited . . . waited . . . She slept. And he didn't dare wake her. Watching her sleep aroused a tenderness in him. He was watching over her . . . and again he had that same feeling he'd had when he'd looked into Hannah's eyes. Love – or whatever it was.

And then he thought, What if it never happened? What if Mary never wanted him the way he wanted her? What would the feeling be then?

Her breathing changed. She sighed, stretched, turned around, her back to him, holding the sheet around her, sighed again in her sleep. He stayed for a few more moments, then crept back to his room.

27

The moment he awoke, he thought of Mary. Then he was out of bed, pulling on a pair of shorts and running downstairs.

She was in the kitchen at the stove, holding Hannah on her hip and heating her bottle. 'Did I wake you?'

He embraced her, embraced her and Hannah.

'Mmm. Good morning.'

He reached for more, but she moved away.

He sat down at the table and leaned on his elbow. She was barelegged, wearing a terrycloth robe and a white towel wrapped around her head. She'd washed her hair, and her cheeks shone.

'I feel wonderful this morning,' she said.

'You look wonderful.'

'I'm making hot cereal. Do you want some?'

'Hot cereal? That's awfully wholesome.'

'I bet you thought I was going to have ice cream for breakfast.'

'With cookies and M&Ms.'

'You would have fit right in with my friends at the workshop. Tom and Marsha eat practically nothing but brown rice.'

'I don't eat brown rice.'

'You would have been proud of me, Jeff. The worst thing I ate in four days was whole-wheat cookies.' She handed him Hannah and the bottle. 'Tom and Marsha are such a neat couple. They live in a house with five other people and they're all dedicated to the stage.'

She was still back there at the workshop.

'They put on plays everywhere. Even if they don't get paid, they're acting. They go to schools, hospitals, even prisons.' She put milk and butter on the table. 'They have a bus, and they call themselves the Oak Street Players.'

'Sounds wonderful,' he said, but he felt like kicking a hole in the Oak Street Players' bus.

'They do theatre in the streets and pass the hat after the performance. They pool their money, everything else, too – expenses, food, everything.'

'Sex, too?'

'Sex is private. We didn't talk about that.' She removed the towel, shook out her hair so it was tangled and loose around her face. It gave her a free, carefree look.

She held her hair out. 'How does that look?'

'Wild.'

'Do you like it?'

'I like wild women.'

'You're not hard to please.'

Then please me . . . I'm ready anytime you are . . .

'Cereal's ready,' she said, taking Hannah.

He gave her a long, earnest look. He was waiting. Excited, but not in a rush. He sprawled out, stretched his legs – body language.

She sat down with Hannah caught between her legs and examined the scrape on the baby's cheek. 'It's still warm. Do you think she'll have a scar there?' She wrapped Hannah in her arms. Her robe fell open and he could see her thighs. Was it a message?

She straightened her robe. The curtain fell. No message. In fact, nothing. No response, no sign, no signals, no body language. Hope fled. He sat there calmly again, lust damped down.

She pulled out the tangles in her hair with her fingers. 'I was surprised about the workshop, Jeff. I thought everybody would be really serious, but most of them were dilettantes, just playing at acting. Not Tom and Marsha. Oh, they're real pros.'

'So what were they doing there?'

'They were there to learn, like everyone else. But they were also looking for people to join their house.' She paused, held out her hand. 'Wait till you hear this. This is my big news. They've invited me and Hannah into the group.'

His whole head got hot. The group. The Group. The professional actors and their professional bus. It was them on one side and him on the other.

'Jeff, do you realize what this will mean to me? It's going to change everything.' She started ticking off on her fingers. 'I'll be able to share Hannah's care. I'll act and earn my own way. I'll be part of a real family. And it's all thanks to you, Jeff.'

'Everything you can do with them, you can do with me. Better, in fact. You want to act, I'll help you. I know how to take care of Hannah. Two heads work better than one. You told me that yourself. We can go to New York or California, anywhere you want to. If we're together, everything will be easy.'

'No.' She looked at him. 'Jeff – no.'

The word echoed in his brain, got stuck there. No . . . no . . . no . . . She'd said no to him before, but never in quite that way. The confidence in her voice! She didn't need him anymore, not the way she had before.

He sprang up. 'What is there, some other guy up there?'

'Another guy?' She picked up Hannah. 'No, I don't want that. Not with you. Not with anybody.'

She sat down beside him. 'Jeff, it's going to happen for you, too, the way it's starting to happen for me. Believe it. After you get to LA—'

He got up, kicked the door open, and walked out in back. The light, the white, intense summer light turned everything into a desert.

When he came back to the house, she and Hannah and all Hannah's things were gone.

28

He stayed away from Mary because he wasn't ever going to see her again. He was cutting her out of his life, erasing her, rubbing her out. She'd call him and he'd hang up. She'd wait outside the house and he'd walk by her. He wouldn't see her, wouldn't hear her. She didn't exist for him.

And then one morning he was there again, standing outside the Belcos'. Two days was all he could take. He went around the side of the house and onto the porch, looked into the kitchen, and saw Mary. She was wearing a green robe and sneakers. She had Hannah in one arm and was moving around the kitchen quietly, murmuring to Hannah, talking to her singsong, unaware that he was there.

She took a dish from the cupboard, and her eyes moved upward, her mouth down, as she filled it. She sat down with Hannah and began to feed her. A firmness came to her face, a lightness to the corners of her mouth.

He stood there, watching, and for a moment it was the beginning again, weeks and weeks ago, and he was seeing her for the first time, and she was there and he was here and they hadn't met yet. And all the possibilities remained.

It could have been the opening of a movie. *Jeff and Mary*. The Great American Love Story – maybe. The hero and heroine hadn't met yet, but everyone in the theatre, unwrapping their candy bars and looking up at the screen, knew they had to meet. There was no movie without the boy and girl meeting, without them falling in love, without troubles and fights and hard decisions and reconciliations. No movie without a happy ending.

He was always seeing people as characters in movies. He was The Great Director, framing scenes, moving people around, distilling characters. Flirtatious Tracy . . . Steady,

Hardworking Danny... Bossy Mrs. Belco ... Mrs. Century, who had outlived her time . . . and Mary . . . and Mary . . . and Mary . . .

Standing there, watching her, he made himself finish . . . And Mary, who wants to live her own way, even with a baby.

Then he walked away.

This time he stayed away for a week. Then he went back. Mrs. Belco stopped him on his way upstairs. 'She's moving. Did she say anything to you? It's none of my business what she does, but I'll still say it, this is my house, not a motel.' None of this said quietly. 'I don't have people here one day and gone the next. My people stay with me.'

He listened. He didn't say anything, but he didn't defend Mary, either.

Mary was waiting for him with her door open. 'I thought that was you.' She half smiled. 'Mrs. Belco gets going, doesn't she?'

It was like he'd been there yesterday, almost like the old days. She had an open box of English cookies, Peek Freans, that she was munching. 'Help yourself,' she said. 'I love these things.'

Her room was a mess, boxes all over. She was packing. 'When's the big day?' he said.

'Wednesday, right before the Labour Day weekend.'

He picked up Hannah. 'You going to miss me? I'm going to miss you.' Hannah grabbed his ear. 'You did that last time, muttface. How about a new trick? When are you going to start walking?'

'She is walking, Jeff. Put her down.'

Hannah stood there wobbling, then staggered across the room, just catching herself on the edge of the bed. 'That's going to get you into the Baby Olympics, Ms. Silver.' He turned to Mary. 'I thought I'd borrow Danny's pickup truck and drive you to that place.'

He'd been thinking about it for days . . .

Scene: Outside of Saratoga they have a flat and no spare tyre. They're stuck in the middle of nowhere and it's getting dark.

You and Hannah sleep in the cab, he says nobly. I'll sleep outside.

But Mary protests. Too buggy. We can sleep in the cab together. Move over on my side, Jeff, where it's more comfortable.

There's not a lot of room, not enough for them to stretch out, but enough for them to get close. He puts his arms around her, his lips against her hair.

Then the kiss. Long, slow kisses. *Close camera work.* She doesn't let him go. Arms around his neck, her face against his.

Another angle: They fall out of the car together. (*Sounds – crackle and buzz of insects.*)

Afterwards she keeps him close.

MARY: How did I stay away from you so long? You were so good and I was so mean. But you don't think I'm mean now, do you? . . .

He sat back on Mary's bed, smiling at her. 'So when do you want to go?'

'Thanks, Jeff, but I don't need a ride. Tom's coming for me.'

Tom? Tom and Marsha. Oh, yeah. He didn't say anything much after that. He stayed awhile, then left with a casual wave.

She called him up Wednesday morning. 'Jeff! I'm leaving today. You're coming over to say good-bye, aren't you?'

It was cool out. Leaves had begun to dry up and fall. He showed up in a denim jacket with a paper flower in his lapel. Mary was on the porch, waiting for him. Hannah was walking, holding on to the railing. As soon as she saw him, she put out her arms to be picked up.

'Oh, am I glad to see you, Jeff,' Mary said. 'Tom's here already. He went to gas up. I was afraid I'd miss you.'

Jeff swung Hannah between his legs. 'What if you don't like them?' He was still trying. 'What if you change your mind?'

'Then I'll do something else. But I'm not going to change my mind. It's going to work out, Jeff.'

'You know, they might hate you.'

'Not a very funny line.'

Mrs. Century came out to say good-bye, manoeuvring cautiously with her cane. She sat down on the porch swing, with her hands on her knees. 'Just let me get my breath. I have to say good-bye to Mary and to my little Hannah.' She took a deep breath. 'I do a little extra breathing every place I go. Now, give that baby to me.' She held Hannah – an old, withered lady holding a little, bouncy rubber ball.

When Tom came back, Mary introduced him. 'This is my friend, Jeff.' Tom was tall, wearing a long Indian shirt, his blond hair hanging down in a long braid. 'Jeff's the one who took care of Hannah for me, Tom. Remember I told you about him?'

Tom had a big, warm, dry hand, and a smile to match. It was hard for Jeff to dislike him. 'There aren't that many guys around who will do what you did, Jeff.'

Mrs. Belco came out. 'Oh, he's here, Mary. Are you leaving now?' She shook Mary's hand. 'Well, come visit us someday. I'm off to work. Did Danny see you to say good-bye this morning?' And she was gone.

Mrs. Century sat with Hannah while Mary, Jeff, and Tom loaded the truck. It was an old school bus actually, painted rainbow colours with the name OAK STREET PLAYERS wavering through a montage of theatre masks and ribbons and birds. Mary dragged the boxes out to the edge of the porch, where Jeff handed them up to Tom in the bus.

When they were ready to go, Tom said, 'You going to come up to visit? There's plenty of room for you, anytime.'

Jeff glanced at Mary. 'I'm going to be away. Travelling.'

'Sure, Jeff is going to visit,' she said. And then to him, 'Just let me get settled first.'

So they'd had a fight and made it up (sort of) and of course he was invited and he could come anytime, but she hadn't really invited him. *Let me get settled first.* A nice way to keep it all vague and off in the future.

Everything was done. Hannah was in the car. Mary hugged Mrs. Century. 'Well . . .' She turned to Jeff. He put out his hand.

'What's that supposed to be, a sanitary kiss? You're not getting away with that, Jeff.' She put her arms around him and hugged him hard.

'The girls are kissing the boys,' Mrs. Century said. 'Nothing new. Nothing's changed. I was the same way myself.'

Jeff watched the bus turn the corner. What did he feel? Nothing. She was gone. The street was still here. The house. The people in it. The sky was still up there. Nothing had changed, and yet he knew everything had changed.

29

After Mary left, he didn't know what to do with himself. Days went by and he didn't do anything. Two weeks in a row, he called Sadie to say he wasn't coming in. 'You want to work, or don't you?' she said.

'Sure,' he said, but he was sick of it, sick of work, sick of the whole world. Anything his parents said irritated him. He stayed away from the house as much as he could. They didn't say that much to him, but just their presence made him feel criticized.

Danny called, but Jeff didn't call back. He did a lot of walking over by the ironworks, where the long steel beams lay rusting in the grass. The weeds grew everywhere, around rocks and through the cracks in the sidewalk. Nothing kept the weeds down.

Mary was like those weeds. She had the strength of weeds. Was it that strength that had drawn him to her from the beginning? Was that what he'd seen in her face, in those large eyes? He'd felt inspired when he saw her, made alive, just as, now, he felt dead.

Where was she right now? What was she doing? He wondered about that when he was walking, or eating, or when he woke up in the morning.

She was coming back – maybe. He kept expecting her. It was the reason he got up in the morning.

He waited and waited. He told himself he was through with her – she was out of his life – but he was obsessed. The more he told himself to stop thinking about her, the more he thought about her. Every morning he thought, Today. Every night it was, Tomorrow.

Suddenly Danny and Tracy announced they were getting married. 'And you're going to be my best man,' Danny said, over the phone. 'Where've you been? You don't come around, you don't answer the phone. Some friend.'

'Married? I didn't know you two were talking.'

'Oh, that. She still doesn't talk to me half the time.'

'What happened to change her mind?'

'Her father got on her case. I always knew we'd get married.'

The wedding was at All Saints. There were a lot of Belcos, but from Tracy's family, the Stauffers, there were only her father, her cousin Dawn, and an older brother who flew in from Atlanta. Dawn was the maid of honour.

He ran into Dawn the night before the wedding at the rehearsal. She was wearing tight jeans and a sweater that left her middle bare. She gave him a dazzling smile. 'I haven't seen you around. How have you been?'

'Good. And you?' As he talked, he looked her over. 'What do you think of this show we're in?'

'I can't believe this is happening. Did you know about it?'

'Sure.'

'Did he tell you everything?'

'Sure did.'

'Not everyone knows. It's not so bad. She can have a couple babies fast and then go to modelling school. Did you know they already have a little apartment?'

He shook his head.

'Yes, right over the Oxford Grill. It's really cute. And convenient. Where's your friend with the baby?'

'She moved.'

'Oh, yeah, I heard that. I heard she went to live with the hippies. Do you miss her?'

'I do sometimes, yes. How about you?'

'I've been having a lot of fun this summer. I've been to the beach almost every day and I worked a little. Keeping the old bod in shape.'

'Looks like you've done a good job. Maybe we can get together sometime.' He didn't know why he said it.

'I'd like that. Do you have any important plans?'

'Uh-huh. I'm going to take a trip – maybe. See the country, get out to California, maybe.'

Her eyes opened wide. 'That sounds fabulous. Want some company?'

'Sure, I'll let you know.'

The morning of the wedding, he sat down in front of the TV, put his feet up, and watched old Flintstone cartoons.

'Aren't you getting dressed?' his mother said.

She got on him, which maybe was what he was looking for. Give him a reason to feel sorry for himself. In his heart he was jealous of Danny, jealous of the way he'd put his life together. No problems for Danny, no fuss, no muss, no questions, no doubts. He got his girl pregnant and he married her. He had two businesses going, restoring old VWs and cutting firewood. And Tracy was working at a market. And she was a hell of a good girl. And they had an apartment over the Oxford Grill. And tonight they'd be at the Bide-A-While Country Motel in New Hampshire, and from now on they could go at it, legally, day and night.

His mother was back with the same question ten minutes later. 'What time do you have to be there? You better get going.'

'Lay off, Mom. It's not going to happen without me.'

She knocked his feet off the couch. 'Stand up. I'm going to cut your hair so you don't look like a wild man.'

He let his hair be cut. Enjoyed it, in fact. Then he got dressed and came downstairs barefoot.

'You're not going to the wedding in your bare feet?'

'Who's going to notice?'

'And that hat?'

'Okay, I'll wear shoes, but the hat stays.' When he left the house, he was wearing the black bowler hat, a red cummerbund, had his Nikon around his neck and was carrying a bamboo cane.

At the church, everyone but the bride and groom was out front. 'Leave it to Jeff,' Mrs. Belco said, pulling up her gloves. 'Leave it to Jeff Orloff to show up at my son's wedding looking like a clown in a circus. Give me that hat. You're not going in there with that.'

Danny's uncle Val put on the bowler hat. It made him look like one of his own pigs.

'Take that off, Val,' Mrs. Belco said.

He pulled it down. 'I like it. It makes me think of FDR's inauguration. Take my picture, Jeff.'

Jeff shot a roll of film of the family, then went looking for Danny, twirling his cane and scanning the crowd as he went.

The ceremony was about to begin, and Danny beckoned him. Standing in front of the priest with Danny, while the bridal march was being played, Jeff let his eyes move across the assembly. Tracy came down the aisle on her father's arm, and he stood there trying to pretend it was Mary coming and he was waiting for her.

30

One day he picked up the phone and called information and got the Oak Street phone number, then dialled before he lost his nerve.

'Jeff! Where are you calling from? Are you in California?'

'Not yet. How are you doing? I thought I'd come up and see you – that is, if you're not too busy.'

'That would be great, Jeff.' And then she hesitated and he knew it was going to be bad. 'When were you planning to come? It wouldn't be convenient right now.'

'Mmm.'

'I'd love to see you,' she said, 'but we're starting a new programme in the schools and I'm away a lot. You could see Hannah, of course. She's home all the time. I'm sure she'd like to see you, but I'm doing schools just about every day.'

'It sounds like things are going right for you.'

'They are, Jeff. Better than I could have hoped. I'm acting, I'm doing plays, I'm learning every single day. And when I'm not around to take care of Hannah, someone else always is. It works out, it really does.'

'So you don't want me to come?'

'I didn't say that. You can come but I don't guarantee I'll be there. I know I won't have a lot of time to spend with you. I thought you'd be setting Hollywood on its ear by now.'

'Any day now.'

'You're not going to do it sitting home, Jeff.'

'Thanks for the advice.' He hung up. The hell with her. She'd rejected him. Again. Ever since she came back from the workshop she'd been rejecting him, and he'd been too obsessed to get the message. Well, he got it now, and he rejected her right back. He was finally through with

Mary Silver, washed clean, emptied out. What remained? Nothing but the need to tell her. He'd cared for her, he'd cared a lot for her. Yes, loved her. He wasn't ashamed to admit it. But that was all gone now. She'd taken care of that. He was crowding her, she'd said, choking her. Well, then choke. He didn't give a damn.

That's what he would tell her, but not on the telephone. Face to face, so there'd be no mistakes. So she'd know exactly what he thought of her. He owed that to himself.

He didn't sleep well that week. He was up late developing Danny's wedding pictures. He caught catnaps during the day.

On Monday, he borrowed Danny's truck. 'Mary again? I thought you were through with her.' Danny had put on some pounds in the few weeks he'd been married. 'Tracy says there's plenty of girls she knows would love to go out with you. I thought you were getting together with Dawn.' He gave Jeff a pitying look. 'Why don't the four of us go out?'

'The keys.' Jeff put out his hand.

'Drive her easy. You look wasted. What've you been doing? No speeding. And if she starts overheating, pull over.'

On the Thruway, he opened the truck up full throttle. After he saw Mary, he'd only go home long enough to pack. Maybe he'd join the service or go out to California, keep going, travel. He was sick of people feeling sorry for him and talking behind his back. Knowing his business. Who didn't know about Mary and him? Damn! He hit his head against the partition, then stepped on the accelerator. Even if he got there in the middle of the night, he'd wake her, and if she was in bed with some guy, he'd throw him out, dump him on his ass.

He drove right into a radar trap. Didn't even know it till he saw the blinking trooper's car ahead of him and the trooper waving him to the side. He shut his eyes and drove by him. What trooper? I don't know what you mean, sir, I wasn't speeding. He fought the urge to look back through the side mirror. If he didn't see the trooper, then he wasn't guilty, was he?

He pressed his foot to the floor, would have pushed it through the floor. There was a sick, soupy feeling in his gut. No strength in his arms. His foot, pressed down on the pedal, shook. The truck did, too. It couldn't take the pounding. It was complaining. It was howling and crying for relief.

Come on, you old junker, move. He leaned forward, urging it on. He cursed the truck and pleaded with it.

A long way back, he saw the flashing red lights. He searched for a turnoff, a place where he could duck behind some trees and hide. The two lanes stretched out ahead, straight as geometry. The shortest line between two points was getting shorter.

He was lost . . . lost without Mary. What was he going to do now? Life, the future, nothing mattered. He felt suicidal – he wanted to shut his eyes and go to sleep and not wake up . . . He pressed the accelerator to the floor.

The trooper came up in the other lane. Jeff swerved in front of him, forced him to fall back. It wasn't him. It was the truck, this old beat-up truck, banging and wheezing, going all over the road. The muffler dropped off. The truck roared like a crazy bull. Go, you old dog. Beat him. Don't let him get me.

He was so tired. His arms . . . his eyes . . . he could hardly keep them open. He closed them, then opened them . . . His father was driving and he was little and sitting in his lap and his father was going full out and laughing his head off . . .

When the trooper finally forced Jeff off the road, he was sitting in the cab laughing, too weak to move.

31

The police gave Jeff the drunk test and searched him for drugs. They booked him for speeding, avoiding arrest, endangering others, driving an unsafe vehicle. They finger-printed him, then locked him in the basement in a window-less cell. They would have allowed him one call – a lawyer or his family – but he said no. He wasn't calling anyone. Tomorrow he'd face the judge.

He pushed the door. No handle on the inside. Bare, dirty walls. A mesh-covered peephole on the door. A single bulb on the ceiling surrounded by metal mesh and a clogged ventilator. Three steps and he crossed the room from end to end. There was no place to go. No room to turn. Nothing to do but wait for morning and think.

Think? That'll be a change for the better.

He looked up at the ceiling, a net of cracks, a spiderweb. His own life was like that, a tangle of emotion. When was he going to get clear? He'd been running all summer, running away from himself, running after Mary. Mary – the girl of his dreams. Talent and beauty and intelligence – smart, too, and fun to be with. He'd seen her clearly, but he could only hear himself mouthing off. Admiration and sex, desperation and lust all mixed together. All summer he had been in a fever of indecision, afraid to make a move for himself, focusing everything on Mary. Wanting her had been easier than figuring out what to do with his own life.

Mary had been running, too, running her own race. He'd been there on the sidelines, cheering her on, passing her the towels and the paper cups of water. Go, Mary! You can do it! Well, she'd done it, found what she needed, left him behind. Sunshine Mary with Hannah in her arms, disappearing over the horizon. Good-bye, Mary.

He took shallow, tentative breaths. He wanted out of here. What was he doing in jail? This is Honest Jeff Orloff. A good kid. Cleancut type. He hit the wall, kicked it with his heel. He was like a horse in a stall. Crowded. Jammed in. Every way he turned, a wall.

How had he ended up here? Easy. He'd been running again. Mary again! Running to see her. Running to tell her off. No, that was just an excuse. He'd wanted to see her again. Still fooling himself. Mary had asked why he wasn't in California. Well, why wasn't he? Scared, that's why. Talk was easy. Doing was hard. 'What do you think, Mary? Not too smart. They're probably going to open up Alcatraz and give me twenty years. What a way to get to California.'

He tossed around on the bed, bored, tired, worried. Afraid of his own thoughts. He concentrated on the sound of his breath rising in his throat. His chest rising . . . falling . . . his stomach sinking . . . his chest rising, swelling, filling out. The air in the cell was thick, damp, heavy with mould. It felt like breathing underwater.

He looked up at the ceiling and saw Mary, a wavery figure appearing and disappearing through the stains and cracks on the ceiling. 'I hope you brought me a cake with a file in it so I can bust out of here.' If he held his head to one side he could just make her out, but if he moved the least little bit she disappeared.

'I bet you think this is bad, right? Wrong. It's the best thing that ever happened to me. I needed to be slowed down. The troopers did me a favour throwing me in the slammer. This is a terrific place. You think it's a cell, but it's really a think tank. No distractions. No TV. No girls. Nothing to take my mind off important things.'

She didn't say anything.

'This is the quietest you've been since I've known you. Since I'm doing all the talking, I'll tell you some other stuff. You know I wanted you a lot. I still want you a lot. That's my trouble. I'm a dreamer. Do I ever see things the way they really are? In my imagination, everything's possible. I have this bad habit of forgetting what's really true. Forgetting there are some things I can never change.'

He jumped up and looked through the peephole. Was someone out there listening to him talk to himself? Next stop, the funny farm. What if they never let him out? What if they came in the middle of the night to beat him?

He flopped down on the bed again. 'You still there, Mary? Don't go away. Where was I? Oh, yes. You and me. And my feelings about you, and who cares? Me. Not you. Oh, you liked me all right. Friends, right? What you said right from the beginning. You told me. Friendship – that was what you offered.

'But I wanted the way Hannah wants. Fact: I wanted you, but you didn't want me. There. I said it. That wasn't so bad. I'll say it again. I want you and you don't want me. At least not now.'

Still hoping, Orloff.

'Okay, maybe not ever. Okay, okay. Not ever. Never.' He sat up. 'Never,' he yelled. The word stuck in his throat. 'I know I created our romance – our love affair. Well, that's upgrading it a bit. Whatever you call it, I did it. On the other hand, you did give me encouragement now and then. Remember those kisses, Mary?'

You're repeating yourself, Orloff.

'Forget the kisses. Forget everything. We're through. Finished. This is the end. The end of the line. And I feel okay, Mary. Not great. But better than when I started this trip. My head is clearer. It's been good talking to you. You don't have to feel sorry for me. Not that you ever did. I have a lot of good stuff to remember – the times we spent together, the things we did. Hannah – I think I'm going to miss her more than I miss you. So whatever it is I'm feeling, it's not an empty feeling. There's something left, something good. And this is my last word. I really did love you, Mary

Silver, in my own crazy way. And Orloff says, if you love somebody, you're never the loser.'

He shut his eyes, then opened them. Mary was gone. All he heard was the hum of motors deep in the building. He needed to sleep, but he couldn't turn his mind off. He was directing again, his mind moving soundlessly up through the walls to a great height. *Long shot:* A laser of light focused in on a solitary figure in a grey cell. Stone on four sides. It was like looking down into an archaeological dig, the tomb opened, and the figure lying there as it had for thousands of years waiting for this moment to arrive . . . An unknown man wrapped in bandages, slowly getting up, standing . . . stretching . . . dusting himself off . . .

The next day Jeff faced the Honourable Judge William Colby in traffic court. Behind him they brought in a kid in handcuffs. The judge had white hair and a ruddy face and a thin mouth like John Wayne. He read the charge in a low droning voice, not looking up. 'How do you plead?'

'Guilty, Your Honour.' He stood up straight and looked right at the judge. No excuses. He had been driving too fast and he hadn't stopped when the trooper flagged him down. As for swerving in front of the trooper, he didn't know what to say about that.

Judge Colby glanced through the papers. 'Were you drinking?'

'No, sir.'

'Using a controlled substance?'

'What, sir?'

'Drugs. You know what I'm talking about.'

'No, sir.'

'Then what the hell was the matter with you?'

'I wasn't thinking. I mean, my mind was somewhere else.'

'Well, where was it?'

Jeff looked around. There were a lot of people sitting in the court. 'It's personal.'

The judge grunted. 'Personal.' He looked up, really looked at Jeff. 'Do personal reasons give you the right to break the law? You're giving me a lot of excuses here. You felt like going like hell so you went like hell. And when the trooper flagged you down you said the hell with that and you kept going. Personal. I'm not impressed. You young people think you can do anything you damn please and then say you're sorry.'

'I am sorry, Your Honour.' He was scared. This judge was a madman, a showman, and a Big Daddy all wrapped up in one black-robed package. He really worked Jeff over, gave him a long lecture about responsibility and death on the highway and disobeying public officers. It was very bad. Humiliating. Even unfair. Was it unfair? Jeff's face burned, but he forced himself to keep looking at the judge. *Take it, Orloff. You've got it coming to you.*

Besides the lecture he got a stiff fine, a mark on his licence, and a final warning. 'I don't want you ever to show up in this court or any other court again.'

The truck had to be hauled home. And more explanations had to be made to his parents and Danny. The repair bills on the truck, the towing charges, and the fine took a big chunk of the money he'd been saving. He stayed on at Sadie's for a couple of months to build up his bankroll again.

It was raining the day he said good-bye to Danny. A fall day, windy and wet, the leaves sticking to the road and the sides of cars. Good-byes were hard, but Jeff felt ridiculously good. For no reason, he was optimistic. Maybe going some-place else was enough right now. He'd already said good-bye to Sadie and to his brother Jules and his sister-in-law, and he'd called Natalie in Bethesda. He felt like a balloon about to be launched.

'California, here I come.'

Danny looked up at the window of his apartment. 'I wish I could get my hands on some of those California cars.'

Jeff felt a twinge of nostalgia for the days when the two of them had done things together. 'Come on. We'll drive out together and you can haul back a couple of cars.'

'No way. With the baby coming—' Danny shrugged.

'Big married man.' Jeff threw his arm around his friend. Danny had always been a step up on him in the maturity department but now Jeff felt on an equal footing, maybe even a little smug. He had never felt so free and unencumbered in his life. 'I'll send you some pictures of me and the starlets.'

His parents came to the bus station with him. His father rubbed the back of Jeff's neck. 'Remember, any time you need us, we're right here.' His mother kissed him and gave him a last hug. 'Now you keep in touch. Don't forget your family. And call home as soon as you get there.'

He was on the bus when he remembered that it had been in the back of his mind to call Mary before he left. Let her know where he was going, say good-bye, but keep it cool. It would be an end. A final shot. *Freeze frame:* Mary, getting the news, then putting the phone down slowly. *Fade out.* Maybe he'd call her on the road or maybe he wouldn't even bother. He put his head back and shut his eyes. He was on this bus because of Mary and he was going to California because of her. Well, she was on Oak Street because of him. They were even. And no more good-byes were necessary. Thinking that, he felt both good and sad.

32

Dear Jeff,

Today is two months that I've been here. I've thought of writing you before, but it seems like this is the first quiet moment I've had. I'm upstairs in my attic room. Yes, in an attic again. I've covered the beams with Indian cloths. I've turned it into a tent, a cave, really. This is my place – the place Hannah and I go to be alone. It's wonderful to have people around me, but I also need that time to myself.

Let me tell you about this place. All through the house there's a wonderful smell of wood fire. It's cosy now up here, but I think I'll need an electric heater this winter. There's a tree outside my window, it's bare now. I've watched it turn from green to red to yellow. This is a big house, a lot of wood moulding and corridors and nooks. It needs painting and some of the porches are sagging, we're supposed to work on it, but Marsha's the only one who sticks with it. In back, the carriage house is big as a barn. We're building a theatre there – long-range plans. Eventually, we want to put on productions for the community.

It's hard to believe where I was at the beginning of the summer and where I am now. So much has happened to me in the last two years. Too much. Sometimes I feel like I'm racing, as if everything is moving too fast. Looking back, sometimes these years seem to stretch forever, and then I get the opposite feeling – that I'm going through life like a rocket. Where am I going to be in a year? Here, I hope.

I love this place. I almost feel guilty saying it. I want to knock on wood. Can it last? Hannah is thriving. She has other children to play with. The big ones watch the little ones. You wouldn't recognize her. You saw her walking, but she's running now. And talk? I can't shut her up.

Jeff, when I think how I almost didn't meet Marsha and Tom and Patti and everyone, how I almost didn't get here . . . I scare myself thinking, What if . . . What if I hadn't gone to the workshop? Do you remember how it happened? I saw that notice for the movie director for you and then you saw the workshop notice for me. What if you hadn't seen it? What if we hadn't wandered into that building? What if it hadn't been so hot? What if we hadn't gone to the park? It's scary to think how life turns on accidents, how we stumble into things. When I look back, when I think back about my life since I went away from home, nothing happened the way I thought it would. Nothing happened the way I would have expected. Nothing.

How strange everything is! Here I am – and where did it begin? I don't mean Hannah, though that's another mystery. I mean me here. Did it begin that day in Mrs. Belco's kitchen? I hardly remember it. I hardly remember you. But there you were when I had the toothache and needed that ride. And what if I hadn't had a toothache? My lucky toothache! You were right about me, Jeff. I've always wanted to be an actress, but when you met me I'd given it all up. And if I hadn't met you I would still be where I was.

And what about you? I tell myself you're busy, doing important things. Where are you? Still home? California? Someplace else? I feel you're very far away. Am I right? I don't mean only in space, though that, too. I mean in friendship. No calls. No letters. Are you okay? Are you busy? Are you famous? Are you romancing another girl? Are you angry? Days when I don't feel good, I think,

Jeff is mad at me. And I don't like that. I don't want you mad at me.

I have a lot of feeling about you. We're friends. I know that makes you mad and I've been tempted to make it more than friends. It would have been easy. I was tempted, and sometimes when I'm feeling lonely and things aren't going well here, I begin to think about Sir Walter Teddybear. But we needed to go our own ways.

I want to hear about you. I miss not having you around to talk to. We had good times together. There's nobody else I miss from that time.

I guess this is a thank-you-Jeff letter. And a don't-forget-me-Jeff letter. And a let's-be-in-touch letter. Write to me. Tell me what you're doing. Come in Jeff, wherever you are.

Love, Mary.

SENTINEL SECURITY SERVICES
2306 Artesia Blvd
Los Angeles, CA, 80076

'Protecting People and Industry Since 1946'

Dear Mary,

If you've bothered to look at the letterhead you'll see that yes, I'm in California, but no, I'm not in security, though I may be soon. I've put in my application to become a security guard. I'm getting very close to the movies. Not the way you would think, but I'll come to that.

Did you know Danny and Tracy got married? Guess who was the best man? I had a few troubles after their wedding. I wasted myself not sleeping. Then I wrecked Danny's truck and spent a night in jail. A long story which I may or may not tell you some time. I hit bottom or what felt like bottom to me. All I know is that it's been uphill since then.

When I got out here I went to all the movie lots and offered myself as a director and screenwriter. Nobody seemed to know who I was and I was getting a little annoyed with these California airheads. Two weeks and I was broke and sleeping in the bushes next to the Freeway. My sister came to the rescue. It was too humiliating to call home after my National Liberation Struggle. While I was waiting for Natalie to send her contribution to the Jeff Orloff Fund, I camped out on the sand. You can't believe how many directors and actors are out here sleeping on the beaches and waiting to be famous.

I finally got on the lots – movie lots, to the uninitiated. Need I add, not as a director. Nor as a screenwriter. Nor as the newest Wonder Kid. I've started my career more modestly. Kitchen worker. This is one of those classic From the Bottom Up Stories, and I'm working my way up rapidly. Already I'm out of the kitchen and on the serving line in the studio cafeteria.

There are so many people involved in making a movie, not just the actors, the cameraman, or the director. There are people putting up the sets, handling the lights, the electricians, the grips, the costume and makeup people. They all come in here. Everyone has to eat, so being on the serving line turns out to be a very influential position. These people are hungry! They depend on me to feed them. And they're grateful for even an extra shot of gravy.

Take Paul Garcia, who's in security. When he comes through the line wearing his grey uniform, leather belt, and holster, I load his plate up good. He takes an instant liking to me, especially on Wednesdays when we serve Swedish meatballs. To show his appreciation, he puts me on to being a security guard. He tells me, 'Put in your application, what have you got to lose? In a few months, you'll be in.' Security guards are the real power behind the scenes. Nobody comes on the lot without passing security. Film crews, actors, stars, even the director has to show his ID. Nobody fools with security.

After security? The next step? Who knows? Maybe I'll move on up to be an assistant to the assistant's assistant. Otherwise known as a gofer. Mysterious are the ways to our famous futures.

I'm going to school two nights a week. Would you believe, acting? I figure if I'm going to be a director, I've got to know something about every job connected to making movies. So don't be surprised if you're sitting in the movies someday and there's Jeff Orloff as part of the posse. And you're going to say, I knew that lad when . . .

You sound good. And so does that little dirtybird, Hannah. Now there's a star. I think about her all the time. Every day when I'm on that serving line and I give someone a hit of squash or mashed potatoes, I think of her. She still packing it in with ten fingers? What a ball she'd have on this serving line. I miss her. You too. A lot more than I'm going to talk about. I'm glad you wrote me, because I wasn't going to write you. When your letter came I was scared, wasn't going to open it. I was afraid it was a cry for help. What if you'd said, I need you, Jeff? I don't know what I would have done.

I think about us, sometimes. I feel like I was really young then. I tried to make everything so simple, tried to pretend we were just a boy and a girl. No connections. No Hannah, no families, just us and our dreams and desires, or should I say, Just me and my dreams and my desires. I wanted Mary. All I wanted was Mary. No, that's not true. I always wanted more.

What I'm trying to say is, right now I'm glad I'm in California and you're in Massachusetts. You're on the

Atlantic and I'm on the Pacific and we're both doing what we want to do. Getting closer to what we want.

But we're going to meet again. One of these months or years, the east will meet the west. What a reunion it will be. We're going to have so much to say to each other, so much to tell. And maybe we'll be able to help each other again. Now that would be neat. Not that you're going to need a lot of help. You've got the talent. I always knew that about you, Mary Silver.

Let's stay in touch.

Jeff

P.S. to Hannah. Remember me? I'm the man in your life. I'm coming back to see you someday, so shape up, kid. The next time around, you better be housebroken and no more mumbojumbo talk. We're going to have an intelligent conversation about life and the stars and the state of the world. So study up and don't forget me, Hannah, 'cause I love you.

M E Kerr
If I Love You, Am I Trapped Forever? £1.75

Handsome, cool, sheer dynamite. If you could be a star at sixteen, Alan was just that. And he had Leah, with her movie-star looks, for a girl friend. So who was this Duncan Stein? Rimless glasses and more interested in reading love poems than joining the sports team . . . So why was everyone suddenly answering all those romantic lonely hearts ads in 'Doomed' Stein's magazine, and why were all the girls wearing anemones?

Alan's disastrous weekend in New York with the father he'd never met before made it all worse, and when Leah dropped him to go with Duncan, Alan began to wonder if *he* was the one who was 'doomed' . . .

Lois Duncan
The Eyes of Karen Connors £1.75

Karen was babysitting for young Bobby and suddenly he was gone. When they found him, everything was all right . . . except that Karen had *known* where he was *before* he was found.

Something like it happened before, when she was very young. Now it was happening again. For no logical reason, she just suddenly *knows* things. And Ron, the good-looking young policeman, wants her help.

This is the power that her mother pretends Karen doesn't have. She can find missing children and there are those who want to stop her using that power. People who are prepared to kill if they have to . . .

Rosemary Wells
When No One Was Looking £1.75

Tennis was Kathy's whole life. She had neither her sister Jody's brains nor her friend Julia's looks. But she did have a phenomenal talent and there seemed no limit to what she might achieve.

Almost everyone wanted Kathy to succeed. The mysterious and attractive Oliver; her coach Marty, because of the publicity; her parents, because of the money and status success would bring; and Julia because . . . well, perhaps because Kathy had once saved her life. Only Jody had doubts.

For Kathy herself, winning became an obsession. Then one day she lost when she really should have won, and the doubts started. And that's when someone decided to give Kathy a helping hand – with tragic consequences.

Barbara Wersba
Tunes for a Small Harmonica £1.75

J.F. is a rebel. She's usually in a bad mood, refuses to study, and from the age of twelve she's dressed like a boy. All of which drives her mother round the bend. Not even Dr Waingloss, her increasingly bewildered psychoanalyst, understands J.F. The only person who does is Marylou, who gives her a harmonica to stop her chain-smoking. It works and she plays well. But J.F. still feels her life lacks purpose.

Then one day she falls madly in love with her poetry teacher. He doesn't know it, and she has a lot to learn about seduction. But from now on she's going to devote all her energy to it. And J.F. has plenty of energy. Poor Harold Murth . . .